PRAISE FOR SIMON FRUELUND

"Beautifully executed, propelled by [Fruelund's] exceptional assurance of form and bone-dry wit."
　　—Olga Ravn,
Booker Prize shortlisted author of
The Employees

"*The World and Varvara* is the type of book you cannot put down."
　　—Preben Rasmussen

"A pure reading pleasure."
　　—Mai Misfeldt

SIMON FRUELUND

The World
and Varvara

Translated from the Danish by
K.E. Semmel

SPUYTEN DUYVIL
NEW YORK CITY

Acknowledgements

The author would like to express his immense gratitude to K.E. Semmel, The Danish Arts Foundation, and to Spuyten Duyvil for making this work available in the English language.

The translator would like to thank the National Endowment for the Arts, whose generous Literary Translation Fellowship nurtured the development of this work during a crucial period, and Pia Møller, who read the earliest draft of this book.

Special thanks to The Danish Arts Foundation for financial support towards the translation and publication of this book.

Danish Arts
Foundation

The original text of The World and Varvara was published by Gyldendal in 2009 as Verden og Varvara.

The cover photo © Camilla Hultén

Library of Congress Cataloging-in-Publication Data

Names: Fruelund, Simon, 1966- author. | Semmel, K. E., translator.
Title: The world and Varvara / Simon Fruelund ; translated from the Danish
   by K.E. Semmel.
Other titles: Verden og Varvara. English
Description: New York City : Spuyten Duyvil, [2023]
Identifiers: LCCN 2023012767 | ISBN 9781959556411 (paperback)
Subjects: LCGFT: Humorous fiction. | Novels.
Classification: LCC PT8177.16.R84 V4713 2023 | DDC
   839.813/8--dc23/eng/20230516
LC record available at https://lccn.loc.gov/2023012767

ONE

Varvara Eng was born on Tuse Næs.

She appears in one of Per Højholt's poems, but she's not his invention. She's not mine, either.

She is real.

She wears orthopedic shoes.

She has a lover named Knud.

She's 79 ½ and lives in an apartment with a panoramic view of the city.

Varvara's full name is Varvara Birgitta Sigismunda Eleonora Margrethe Sophia Eng.

She was conceived in the basement pantry at Adserbølle Manor.

With her father, the count, standing and her mother, a maid, seated on one of the shelves, the jars of preserves jangled and clinked and shifted.

When the jars began to fall and the scent of blackcurrants filled the cool room, the maid ordered her master to keep going.

She'd helped to pick and conserve the berries, and afterwards she herself had to clean it all up.

Varvara and I have our first meeting on a Tuesday in July.

We sit on opposite ends of a red and white-striped sofa.

We drink a white tea that Varvara says comes from China.

I turn on the recorder and ask a single, rather cautious question, and soon she's telling me about her early childhood.

I once read that it was so cold at Lenin's funeral that the musicians had to wipe their instruments with vodka so their lips wouldn't stick.

That's about how chilly it was on the January day some eighty years ago when Varvara entered the world.

It was 7 degrees Fahrenheit, and windy.

Down in the basement, the boilerman (who was also the gardener and had a club foot) moved like a pendulum back and forth between the coal cellar and the furnace, and around the house the staff made sure to stoke the woodstoves that, a few years earlier, had been supplemented with radiators.

A doctor had been called in from Holbæk, but as time passed, and the contractions grew so strong and frequent that Varvara's twenty-two-year-old mother nearly passed out, the count grew increasingly nervous.

In the end he sent for the cook.

Approaching the mustard-yellow four-poster bed where the young countess lay, she shot the count a condescending glance.

He asked one of the maids to help out, and then with pensive steps went down the wide, thickly carpeted stairs.

He continued into his beloved smoking room, where long Meerschaums and porcelain pipes hung on the walls, and there he sat reading *Statstidende*, the *Berlingske Aftenavis*, and *Holbæk Amts Venstreblad* (which, though liberal, was at least local), and every so often he got up and walked to the window to watch for the doctor.

Now and then he went to the stairwell and tried to determine how things were coming along by listening to the groans from above.

The doctor never showed, and he wasn't found until his body washed ashore at Orø several weeks later.

Apparently, his car had broken down, and he'd attempted a short-cut across the ice.

A writer is helping Varvara Eng write her memoirs, and that writer is me.

It was an arrangement brokered by my publisher.

It was accompanied by a check (which I immediately cashed) along with a few admonishments (that I barely heard), and I've promised to complete the manuscript in eight weeks.

The book is to be published when Varvara turns eighty.

—I want a writer, she'd told my editor. I want someone who knows how to lie without being exposed.

Varvara Eng has lived nine lives.

In the first she did everything that was expected of her.

In the second she did nothing of what was expected.

In the third she had four children.

In the fourth she became an actress and shocked the landed gentry of Zealand.

In the fifth she took a nap.

In the sixth she kept getting married.

In the seventh she remained unmarried but had an almost unbroken chain of affairs.

In the eighth she became a morphine addict, a Christian, and an expert on roses.

In the ninth she died of boredom.

Varvara Eng has a rooftop terrace where she grows more than thirty types of roses, and the second time I visit her that's where we sit.

We drink iced tea on the porch swing until four o'clock and, later, Campari and orange juice.

We are able to see Frederiksberg Park, Søndermarken, and most of Vesterbro.

On the table before us rests a large, cloth-bound box containing old photographs.

The count's daughters from his first marriage had lean, pale faces and watery eyes.

Only the son, Clifford, inherited his father's dark complexion.

At age thirty-five their mother, the first countess, was admitted to the State Mental Hospital in Nykøbing, never to be released.

Years of mood swings had come to a head when she drove her car into the fjord with baby Cliff in the backseat.

Shortly before the accident, she'd gambled away one of the tenant farms in a card game.

Exactly when the count had begun to take notice of the young maid from Svebølle, no one knew for sure.

Varvara Eng always wears dresses. She has liver spots and wrinkles and thick eyeglasses, but when she removes the glasses, I recognize the seventeen-year-old girl in the photographs.

The expression in her eyes is surprisingly tender.

Her head is small and her neck long.

Her legs are relatively stocky, her torso ample and short.

She's a little swaybacked.

On bad days she has a certain resemblance to an ostrich. On good days she looks like a goddess.

When she was a fifteen-year-old riding through Adserbølle forest, a lumberjack sawed off the tip of his index finger.

A few years later, a count from Langeland sent her roses every week for seven consecutive months.

—Beauty is such a strange thing, she says. I'm not sure one should trust it.

Every one of her husbands cheated on her, she tells me, except for the one she betrayed on their honeymoon.

The third time I visit Varvara, Knud opens the door.

He has white hair that he slicks back over his scalp, a cleft in his chin, and a little silk hanky around his neck.

—There's our young poet! Come in, come in! We're going for a drive!

Knud owns a dark green Bentley with light brown leather upholstery.

He wears black driving gloves, and Varvara and I sit in the backseat.

Every now and then Varvara points at an apartment building or a massive industrial park and sighs:

—In the old days it was much nicer around here. There were fields.

—What a fucking idiot, Knud grumbles when a semi moves into the passing lane.

—Language, my dear, Varvara says.

—He cusses like a Turk, she says to me.

—Have you ever heard a Turk cuss? Knud asks.

Varvara smiles:

—I guess there's quite a lot you've never experienced.

I've prepared a number of questions, but only manage to ask the first before Varvara says:

—Knud, why don't you tell Pelle about the time you met Jackie Onassis?

Knud has been a diamond trader for more than fifty years.

He's been a regular at Hovenierstraat in Antwerp and 47th street in New York. He's visited mines all around the globe.

He's Jewish, but not a believer.

—I believe in Varvara, he says.

—No, you don't! she says. You believe in yourself.

He tells me about Antwerp: The Jews dressed in black, the Sikhs in their colorful turbans, and the European businessmen in suits from Saville Row.

—Knud's mother stitched their entire fortune into his clothes.

—Yes, I learned that early on: Diamonds are a Jew's best friend.

In an Australian diamond mine, he met an American trader by the name of Maurice.

He lived in an enormous apartment on Fifth Avenue, and when Knud visited him for dinner a few months later, a stylish woman, who introduced herself as Jacqueline, met him at the door.

She explained that Maurice was running a little late and offered Knud a drink.

They spent half-an-hour alone, and she politely inquired about Denmark and his impression of the United States.

—I thought you knew, Maurice said afterwards. Everyone knows. It's a huge scandal here. We live together, and we're not married. Technically speaking, I'm still married to my wife.

—So what was she like? I ask.

Knud smiles.

—It was a bit like being with a black and white photograph. I can see why John F. started chasing after Marilyn.

We have lunch underneath a patio umbrella in the courtyard at Søllerød Inn. Varvara and Knud order caviar, and I eat scallops.

We drink a white wine called Meursault, and Knud tells me about the time he was on safari with Zaire's President Mobutu.

—He was an absolute criminal, Varvara says.

—Oh, he wasn't so bad, Knud says. In fact, he was quite friendly. And I really liked his leopard-skin hat.

That same day I got a reminder from the Unemployment Office.

They write that I've been expelled, effective immediately.

They've discovered that I've engaged in artistic work during my period of unemployment, and now they're requesting I pay back 100,000 kroner.

In the spring, so their reasoning goes, I published a book of flash fiction. My advance was 4,148 kroner, and the last time I checked, 372 copies had been distributed.

—Which unfortunately isn't the same thing as *sold*, my editor emphasized.

Varvara naps in the backseat.

We pass Hillerød and drive north, Grib Forest on one side and Esrum Lake on the other.

I sit in the front seat.

I'd hoped we could pay a visit to Adserbølle, but Knud and especially Varvara would rather drive to Rågeleje.

—If you really want to, we can drive there someday, Varvara said. It's just a horrid old manor house. Let's do it on a rainy day.

—Any money in being a writer? Knud asks.

—Not really, I say. Not for me anyway.

—If you ever need to make some extra cash, just let me know. Every so often I need a courier.

I think about Rimbaud, who gave up writing poetry and became a weapons smuggler in Abyssinia. It's said he died a wealthy man.

Knud was born in Copenhagen in 1932. His father was a merchant. They owned an entire block of Bredgade near the Russian Church.

In 1940 they fled to Haifa.

—My parents hated being there. They thought it was too hot and too filthy. They were cultivated people. They were Europeans. As soon as the war ended, we returned to Copenhagen. We definitely thought the Germans got off much too easy. They could've given us Berlin. Or Cologne. Or Vienna! What good was a parcel of desert teeming with unfriendly Bedouins? All because of an old book?

He smiles.

—That probably makes a guy like you happy, doesn't it? The power of literature!

—Don't listen to him, I hear from the backseat.

—Are you awake, my love?

—Oh yes. Are we there anytime soon?

Knud's summerhouse is comprised of three black, wooden cottages with thatched roofs, and a swimming pool in the center. The pool is near the slope and offers a view of the Kattegat.

A VW Beetle convertible is parked at the house.

—Oh, how I need a swim in the sea, Varvara says.

—I think my granddaughter Emma is here, Knud says.

We walk inside, and he finds a pair of bathing trunks and a towel for me.

He follows Varvara upstairs, and when they return ten minutes later, she's wearing a purple bathing suit patterned with red flowers.

I notice her arms. They are fleshy and not particularly wrinkly.

Knud is slender for a man his age, and there's a swirl of gray hair on his chest. He's wearing a pair of tight black swim trunks.

Walking down the path to the beach, we run into Emma and her friend.

They are in their early twenties.

They are suntanned.

They're wearing bikinis.

Knud introduces me, and they smile.

The girlfriend's name is Knirke.

Varvara and I stand on the second sandbar talking while Knud heads out toward the third.

—What's your earliest memory? I ask.

—Oh, I don't know. I remember a horse running amok on a plowed field. My mother sitting on a gig that's bouncing up and down. I also remember that Cliff bit a dachshund's ear. We had these enormous hunts, you know. I remember the blood running down his cheeks.

Varvara's first husband was Baron Henrik of Søholm.

He was one of the count's hunting buddies.

When it wasn't hunting season, they played cards and drank, and one winter night in 1946 the count lost half of his possessions.

The baron, though, was willing to cut him a deal.

Varvara was eighteen, and although the farm manager's son, Ditlev, had inserted three fingers inside her, she was still a virgin.

The baron was missing a finger on his right hand.

His forehead extended across his scalp and came

within two inches of his nape, and he had a pointy, rather porous nose.

—I remember how on our wedding night, after the baron had fallen asleep, I lay thinking about Ditlev. Why hadn't I let him? It would've been far more dignified. Henrik's experiences came from prostitutes and the servant girls who rarely lasted more than a few months. He treated me more or less just like them, but I lasted a year and a half. Thank God he was sterile.

When we get back to the house, Emma and Knirke are lying by the pool. They've removed their bikini tops.

Emma's on her back with her eyes closed, and Knirke's on her stomach, reading.

I see the dimples on her lower back, one above each cheek.

Knud raises his brow.

—How about a drink?

The girls have gone grocery shopping, and Varvara and I sit on wicker chairs close to the slope.

Knud's prepping the grill.

Down on the road I see a beach buggy passing by, and a motorboat heading toward Gilleleje.

Behind the motorboat soars a large bird, a cross between a seagull and an osprey.

—Look at that, Varvara says. I think it's a fulmar.

In all secrecy, Varvara contacted the family lawyer.

He was a tall, bespectacled man who attended the occasional party at Adserbølle.

She had heard he'd gotten a convicted murderer out of prison.

He ought to be able to get her a divorce, right?

He greeted her kindly in his office on City Hall Square and told her that, legally, nothing stood in the way of her divorce.

When he heard why she'd married, he smiled and suggested she travel abroad for a while.

He asked whether she had family or others she could visit, and since she didn't, he offered to contact an English editor whom he'd met a few years earlier in Nürenburg.

Three weeks later, Varvara departed Søholm with two suitcases and a purse.

She left behind a note to Henrik, who was in the forest, and never again set foot in that house.

One of the farmhands drove her to the station.

Many hours later, when she reached Esbjerg, a heavy fog lay on the sea. Her departure was delayed for an indeterminate period of time, and as she was walking on the wharf, she fell into conversation with an American Naval officer.

He invited her on board his ship.

—He was so handsome, Varvara says. Though we only spent a few hours together, he opened up a whole new world for me.

All the way to Harwich she laid naked in her bunk.

I go inside and call Johanne.

—It's a long session today, I say. Maybe we can go to the movies tomorrow instead?

—That's okay. I'm sitting here reading Tranströmer. He is just so amazing!

Johanne's twenty-nine years old and a poet.

We met at a reading a few years ago.

For more than a year we've talked about moving in together.

We've talked about having a baby.

Johanne is afraid she won't have enough time to write.

She's afraid she won't be a good mother.

—Consider Sylvia Plath, she says. That was a disaster. Consider Thomas Mann and Virginia Woolf and James Joyce. They were all such awful parents. It's a very big decision.

—I don't think Woolf had any children.

—She committed suicide, for god's sake!

Johanne smokes twenty-five cigarettes a day and is a vegetarian.

She doesn't understand why I've agreed to write a book about Varvara.

—Think about what it'll do to your own work, she says. Think about your reputation.

Knirke and I sit across from each other.

We eat freshly dug new potatoes smothered in crème-fraîche, which Varvara calls get-fresh cream.

She says she prefers tenderloin of the lamb over that from a pig or cow.

Emma talks about her studies.

She's training to be a midwife.

Before that she studied medicine, but in the middle of a dissection she fainted onto the cadaver.

She has light blond hair cut into a page and speaks so fast it can be difficult to hear what she's saying.

She tells us about a woman who wouldn't give her name.

She showed up one Thursday evening while Emma was on duty at the hospital, and within an hour she'd given birth.

Within another hour she'd left the hospital.

She gave the child up for adoption.

—Was she a prostitute or drug addict or something like that? I ask.

—She looked ordinary: well dressed, neat, no needle marks or anything. It'd be easier to imagine her working at a bank.

—How strange that must be, Varvara says.

—The nurses were really sad when child services came and picked him up. They'd grown pretty fond of him.

Knud opens another bottle of wine.

—If you need to get home tonight, Pelle, you need to let me know soon.

—Stay, Varvara says. You can have your own cottage.

We hear music and loud voices from a house farther down the road.

—Who's having a party? Emma asks.

—I think it's Henning or one of his kids.

—Gut-Henning, Varvara says.

—Gut-Henning? I ask.

—He's the CEO of a company that sells pig intestines. They're the world's largest producer.

—That sounds yummy, Knirke says.

—He once told me that if they made one large sausage from a single year's production, it would wrap around the globe twenty times.

Knud tells the story of a woman he once met at a Zürich hotel.

She was a journalist with *The Times*, and after two months' residency in Africa, she'd gone to Switzerland for a little rest and relaxation.

This was during the war in Biafra.

Knud was in his mid-forties and recently divorced.

He'd traveled quite a bit in Africa himself and had met many of the new Black presidents.

They ate a few dinners together, and before he travelled on to Paris, she asked him if she could contact him again.

When, later, she called him at his home in Rungsted, he answered her questions the best he could.

She wanted to know, for example, what Milton Obote's favorite make of car was.

A few years later they met for lunch in London, and when she picked up her bag to go to the bathroom, he noticed a small silver pistol.

He left the restaurant immediately and never heard from her again.

—Was she beautiful? Varvara asks.

—Of course, Knud says, grinning. Not as beautiful as the ladies in the present company, but yes, she was attractive.

—Did you ever check to see if she really was a journalist? Knirke asks.

—I did not, Knud says. For some reason, I trusted her.

Emma shows me around in the middle cottage. She finds a towel and some bed linen.

—Do you need anything else?

—I don't think so, I say. But thanks.

She remains standing in the doorway a moment.

—Well, sweet dreams, she says.

An Ejler Bille painting hangs on the wall.

The bed is old, but the mattress is brand new.

There's a large window from which I can see Knirke brushing her teeth inside the house next door.

She has coffee-colored hair that falls nearly to her shoulder blades.

One shoulder blade moves in rhythm to her toothbrushing.

She must have noticed me because she suddenly turns and waves.

I wave back.

I wake to my cell phone buzzing.

It's five minutes past nine o'clock.

It's Andreas Bovin, my editor.

—How's it going? he says. Moving forward?

—We're holed up at a summerhouse in Rågeleje.

—Excellent! I look forward to reading something. Will you send me some pages one of these days?

I promise I will.

He has sent me a stack of interview-based biographies that I've thumbed through, and he's told me that the publishing house has high expectations for this project.

—It's a good story, he said. She has led an incredible life.

There's not a cloud in the sky.

Knud is sitting in a black Hugo Boss morning robe and reading *Berlingske Tidende*.

A plate with a half-eaten pastry and a cup of coffee is resting on the grass.

Varvara is inside somewhere singing with a surprisingly deep voice:

Row, row, row your boat
Gently down the stream
If you see a crocodile
Don't forget to scream

She screams.

Knud shakes his head and puts down the newspaper.

Knirke and Emma join us.

—What happened?

—Nothing. I think she was just on the phone with her son.

Knirke has one foot up on the seat, holding her leg while sipping coffee.

Emma tells of a trip to Malaysia.

She tells of Kuala Lumpur, Kuantan, and Penang.

—It all sounds marvelous, Varvara says. We should go to Indonesia, Knud, don't you think?

—Malaysia, Emma says.

Knud grunts and glances up from his newspaper.

—Don't they have tsunamis and Al Qaeda there?

—But that's what makes it so exciting, isn't it?

Varvara looks at Emma.

Knirke and I look at each other.

—I don't think that's what makes it so exciting. Above all it's the Malaysians. They are unbelievably friendly.

—Yes, Varvara says, but the adventure, all the

dangers, and the small sinewy men … Tigers, surely there are tigers in Malaysia!

The English editor had a daughter who was one year younger than Varvara.

She was named Vanessa and had freckles.

She had recently been accepted into the Royal Academy of Dramatic Art and introduced Varvara to her friends.

Varvara met a young actor.

Varvara met a lord.

Varvara met a star cricketer.

Varvara met an Indian professor.

Varvara met a waiter.

When the divorce was finalized, she got her own apartment. She got a driver's license and a little sports car.

She began taking lessons from an older actress.

—You have talent, my dear, she said, but your English is ghastly. It sounds as though your mouth is full of custard. Is that really how you talk in Hamlet's own country?

Varvara and I take a walk on the beach.

She has wound a red silk shawl around her hair.

It's fluttering in the wind.

I walk around with my recorder in one hand and the microphone in the other.

She tells me about Vanessa, who fell in love with a former Royal Air Force pilot. He was a terrible alcoholic, and one winter morning he was found dead outside his front door, his keys in his hand.

She tells me of a London under reconstruction, about Sundays on the Thames and an affair with a member of the House of Commons.

She tells me she once saw Winston Churchill exit a restaurant.

—He looked like a man who'd won it all and lost it immediately.

On our way back we run into Knirke.

She's got a camera.

She asks whether she can snap a few pictures of Varvara.

—Of course, Varvara says, smiling.

She poses.

Knirke fixes her shawl or asks her to lift her head.

I go on ahead and fetch my bathing trunks and my towel, which I left behind a dinghy.

Neither of them notice me change my clothes and walk out into the waves.

When I return a little later, they're still taking photographs.

I sit down on the dinghy and wait.

Knirke is a photographer.

She's a student at the Academy of Fine Arts.

She was born on Anholt and went to gymnasium in Copenhagen.

Her first exhibition just opened and consists of images of her family.

Varvara's mother was born on a little farm just outside of Svebølle.

When quite young she was a maid at Dragsholm Manor, where the count took notice of her at a party.

A year later she was hired at Adserbølle.

The first twenty years of her life she was bullied and bossed around, and the next sixty years she bullied and bossed others around.

She convinced the count to go on safari in Africa.

She convinced him to buy a Jaguar.

She was the first woman in the Holbæk police district to get a motorcycle license.

When Varvara departed for England, her mother was the one who convinced Henrik of Søholm, a man approximately her own age, from laying claim to Adserbølle.

The following years she paid him a visit about once a month.

When he died in a hunting accident on Langeland five years later, she and the count were both present.

—It's as though we lost a family member, the count told a reporter from *Kalundborg Folkeblad*.

I've borrowed a laptop computer from Knud and sit under an umbrella transcribing the tape.

Knirke and Emma are lying beside the pool.

Varvara is taking a midday nap, and Knud has driven to Rungsted to pick up some documents.

Knirke is lying on her back.

I listen to Varvara's dark, raspy voice in my headphones and think that she could just as easily be a man.

I start and stop the tape, my sweaty fingers gliding around on the computer keys.

At one point, Emma stands and walks into the house to the left.

At one point, Knirke gets up and leaps headfirst into the pool.

She swims a few laps and then rests at the pool's edge close to me.

I can see her moving her lips, and I lift off my headphones.

—Can you swim underwater?

—Um, yeah.

—Do you want to see who can swim the farthest?

Cliff visited Varvara in London.

He was on his way to the United States to study agriculture.

As the only son, he was slated to take over Adserbølle's 10,479 acres.

He got drunk and ran off with one of her male actor friends already on the second night.

He turned up a week later and declared that he would never return to Denmark.

When the actor, one month later, fell for a 17-year-old tailor's apprentice with beautiful white hands, Cliff continued on to Iowa, and a few years later he married a countess ten years younger than him.

To Varvara's astonishment she resembled the young tailor: a boyish figure with crooked eyes, brown hair, and cream-colored skin.

—They asked whether I would like to stay up here a few more days, I say.

—That's totally fine, Johanne says. I don't know if I have the energy to go to the movies anyway. I've begun to write. I've written three poems today alone. They're really, really political. I've never written anything so hard-hitting. They're also really, really feminist.

—Sounds cool, I say.

Johanne has written three books that have garnered positive reviews (far more positive than mine), and already speaks of her "oeuvre."

She likes to be tied up, and even though I actually don't feel much like it, I sometimes tie her to the bedposts.

Then I ignore her and make coffee or tea or take a shower or go shopping, and she's usually completely beside herself when I return.

Her parents both teach Danish literature in gymnasium.

They are very proud of her.

They are very careful also to praise my books.

We eat at Jan Hurtigkarl's restaurant in Ålsgårde.

I've borrowed one of Knud's light-blue shirts to go along with my old threadbare jeans and a pair of sneakers.

Knud orders a bottle of wine that costs more than $130 dollars.

I catch sight of Baron Otto Reedtz-Thott at the other end of the restaurant. He's with two couples and a tall, dark-haired woman I assume is his wife.

Emma and Knirke seem totally unimpressed.

We sit at the window with a view of Sweden.

The African-inspired cuisine is served on palm leaves.

There's banana in the first course and yams in the dessert. Among other things, we eat antelope in chocolate sauce with okra parfait.

Emma gives the food high praise.

Knirke smiles.

I praise the view.

Varvara tells us about a three-starred Michelin restaurant in Paris where she once ate birds' nests

—Did we go there together? Knud asks.

—It was before your time. Three or four marriages before you, in fact.

—How many times have you been married? Knirke asks.

—Five times, give or take

—Give or take? Emma says.

—If it lasts under three months, then I don't think it counts.

—We're not married, Knud tells me. I don't have the guts. Varvara has a tendency to kill off her husbands.

—Yes, I think too highly of Knud to want to marry him. He survived Hitler, that was a bit of an achievement. There's no reason to tempt fate, is there?

I look at Knirke.

Her gaze has slowed down. It lingers on mine a little longer than it needs to.

—Do you want to drive? she says when we're standing beside Emma's Beetle.

—I don't actually have a driver's license.

—*Can* you drive?

—Not really, I say.

—Hop in.

I walk toward the passenger seat.

—Not there, she says. *There.*

I walk around the car and sit behind the wheel.

She sits down beside me.

—Then I'll teach you.

She gives me a quick lesson, and I turn the key.

The car stalls.

—You're letting off the clutch too fast. Try again.

I try a few more times.

—You say that you haven't had a lot of success as a writer, and you can't drive a car. There must be something you're good at?

I smile.

I try again, and the car rolls slowly toward the driveway.

Varvara met her second husband at the British Museum.

She stood observing a little terracotta figure of a naked woman riding a pig.

—What do you think? someone said.

She looked up and caught sight of a smiling young man with reddish-blond hair.

—I am wondering why she's riding sidesaddle.

—Yes, it must be hard to hold her balance.

—But I like it. What's that on top of her head?

—It looks like a bucket or something?

—And some kind of veil above?

—Something like that, yes.

They looked at each other.

—Phil, he said and offered his hand.

Knirke and I walk into the waves.

It's one of the last white nights of the summer, and she's not wearing a bikini top.

There's something strange about her nipples.

—My children will have to drink through straws, she says.

I look a little closer at them.

They're turned inward.

—See, here they come, she says. The cold does it.

—They're nice, I say quickly and immediately become more embarrassed.

—Thanks, she says. I've gotten used to them.

From the bathroom window I see Varvara standing and doing tai-chi at the edge of the slope.

There's a light mist over everything.

The sea is calm.

I walk in and lay down behind Knirke.

She opens her eyes, smiles, and closes them again.

I cup my hands around her breasts.

I believe she's sleeping when she suddenly says:

—I am leaving tomorrow. I'll be gone for a while.

I hold her closer to me and feel one nipple pop out between my fingers.

—Where are you going? I say.

Not until much later does Varvara realize that Phil's specialty is picking up foreign girls.

When his colleagues went to lunch, he went to the museum.

He had an apartment downtown, and now and then

he succeeded in luring a girl home and being back at the office before his boss noticed.

The boss was his father.

The family firm imported tea and spices from India and China, and his grandfather founded it himself.

—Phil was terribly charming. It's so disarming when people really believe in themselves. Also when they have no reason to. Maybe *especially* when they have no reason to. I mean, he was a redhead, of rather average gifts, lazy as a toad, and I was completely sold. Isn't that amazing?

We sit near the slope.

Knirke and Emma have gone to the beach, and I think they've been gone for quite a while

—He had some kind of effect on my reproductive system. It was as if it was all wide open and fluttering. I got pregnant the very first time we were together.

Knirke says:

—I don't want to hear anything about Johanne or about any of the girls you've been with. You can tell me *one* story, and then I'll tell you one, and then I don't want us to talk anymore about it. It can become such a heavy burden.

—That's all right, I say. You start.

She tells me about her first love.

She'd had a crush on a particular boy for several years when, at a 7th grade class party, he approached her and asked her to dance.

—I was so shocked that I decked him. And I punched him really hard. He fell backward. When I realized what I'd done, I ran sobbing out to the schoolyard where I sat angrily biting a soccer ball when he came and found me. He got a black eye, and we dated for a year.

I tell her about a plastered woman who once hit on me thinking I was a girl.

I was fifteen.

Cliff and the countess never had children, and so Varvara's son William is the one running Adserbølle.

He doesn't approve of his mother's lifestyle.

He doesn't approve of his siblings.

He wears tweed and argyle-patterned clothing and knee-highs and drives a Land Rover and a Jaguar.

He speaks English with his wife and his children, and each autumn he hosts a huge Hubertus hunt.

He beats his dogs.

—When his father and I divorced, he refused to see me for several years. He has never forgiven me.

I go inside to use the bathroom.

As I'm standing at the toilet, I spot a light-blue pill underneath the shower curtain.

I wash my hands and pick it up.

It's got a strange shape.

I don't know what to do with it, and I end up putting it in my pocket.

Knirke and I drive to Gilleleje and buy plaice at the harbor.

She tells me about her trip: She's going to visit a number of expat Danes along with an anthropologist. They will be gone for two months.

We eat ice cream.

I reach for my pants and pull the blue pill from my pocket. I show it to Knirke.

—What is it?

—I think it's Viagra.

She puts her hand on my cock.

—So it must be Knud's, huh?

—I guess.

—But don't you think he might need it?

I crawl out of bed.

—You're right. I should put it back.

Knirke pulls me down again.

—Not in that condition, she says. That would be cruel.

The next day I tie Johanne to the radiator (it's cold, it's still summer) and go out to drink a beer.

I meet my friend Sune whom I went to Writer's Academy with.

We drink a couple beers and then we meet Jonas, who was in the class right behind us, and an hour later I come to think of Johanne.

I hurry home to her.

She tells me that I'm the biggest asshole she's ever met, but she still wants to fuck.

I don't feel like it.

I break up with her.

I don't know what to say, so I tell her that I am no longer in love with her.

She tells me that I'm the biggest asshole she's ever met.

I leave.

I text Knirke and tell her that I've broken up with Johanne.

Ten minutes later I get a response:

:-) hope it wasn't
too hard. we've just
arrived in Catania.
it's more than a 100
degrees here.

Two

He can see Strombolicchio from his office.

He has bought a cheap pair of binoculars in one of the tourist shops down at the harbor, and through it he can see people walking over there.

There's a stairway with over 200 steps carved into the cliff.

There's a little white lighthouse.

Every so often a cruise ship sails close by.

The one hundred fifty-foot-tall cliff towers above the sea a couple miles to the northeast.

He has read somewhere that it's a plug of congealed lava from a long since eroded volcano.

He is sixty-five.

He has lived on the island of Stromboli for four years.

He has published seven poetry collections, two essay collections, six novels, and has received the Academy's biggest prize.

His wife lives in Denmark most of the year.

He, however, has never really felt equally at home anywhere.

The house he has rented has split levels, heavy mahogany shutters, mint-green and sand-colored floor tiles, and hand-decorated doors.

There's a small black beach at the end of the property.

There are around 400 permanent residents on the

island and no cars—only small three-wheeled Apes and golf carts.

There's an active volcano.

Over time he has learned enough Italian to get by in the shops, but not enough to read a newspaper.

He's become good friends with a German sculptor.

The German is almost fifty, has a pigtail, and ambles around the island with a slightly rocking, optimistic gait.

He drops by at all hours of the day and shouts up to him from the beach below the house.

Then they play chess or sit on the terrace and glance up at the volcano or take a walk into the city and eat homemade ice cream at a café near the harbor.

Christmas he usually spends in Denmark.

That way he can nurture the few friendships that have survived a long life in the service of literature, and what's left of his family.

He has two daughters.

Sometimes he meets a couple of Danish tourists on the island.

Mostly they are people his own age.

With walking staffs and small backpacks they come to climb the volcano, and after a few days they usually continue on to Vulcano or Panarea.

On the way, they catch a glimpse of the house in which Ingrid Bergman lived during the filming of *Stromboli*.

He saw the film on television once at the beginning of the 1980s, and he saw the crater the first time he visited the island.

Now he can see the eruptions from his terrace, the reddish smoke, the ash, the lava bombs, all of the more or less constant fireworks that are termed Strombolian activity.

From a boat he has seen the place where the lava runs down the volcano's side.

Sometimes a young writer pays him a visit.

An anthropologist visited him in August.

He arrived on the *aliscàfo* one Saturday morning accompanied by a female photographer.

He was in his late thirties, and she was a little younger.

On the way out to Piscita, she sat beside him in the golf cart and watched Strombolicchio.

A few times, she raised her camera and lowered it again.

He and the man spent most of the day on the terrace, but after having taken quite a few pictures, the photographer went down to the beach.

They saw her standing on the breakers in a turquoise bikini.

He watched her as he tried to say something intelligent about his lack of connection to his homeland.

For some time she stood staring in the direction of Strombolicchio, and there was something about her posture and gaze that made him think she knew precisely what was coming.

In the middle of the afternoon the wind picked up, and when he said goodbye to them at five p.m., he could see with his own naked eye the spray of white foam along Strombolicchio's sides.

On Sunday he bumped into them at the grocery store as the man was buying cigarettes.

They told him the hydrofoil had been grounded.

The woman asked him how long it usually took.

He told them how Virgil put Aeolus, the god of wind, in a cave on Stromboli.

He added, however, that the large boat that sails between Napoli and Milazzo is usually able to dock.

On Monday evening, he and the German ate at the pizzeria below the church, and suddenly he realized the couple sitting in a confidential, almost intimate conversation a few tables away were his two visitors.

When he awoke the next morning, he noticed at once that the wind had settled down.

His customers are usually wealthy women between the age of forty and sixty.

If they are younger, they're typically extremely unattractive, and if they are elderly, the circumstances are typically unusual.

The oldest he has ever slept with was 82.

Her husband had recently passed away, and she lived

alone with a maid and a driver in a 2,600-square foot apartment close to Buckingham Palace.

—Oh, David, she said when he thrust himself into her, rough me up a bit, will you?

David is his nom de plume.

He lives on Blenheim Crescent just across from the bookstore that, according to the store itself, was the inspiration for the one in *Notting Hill*.

He is thirty-seven.

His parents are doctors, and he managed to retake the first year of med school four times before he ran away.

Shortly before, he'd met a successful Danish businesswoman at the NASA night club, and she installed him in an apartment close to Abbey Road where, during lunch breaks, he would eat sashimi directly from her pussy or penetrate her anally.

She was married to a Canadian psychology professor and had three children.

She was ten years older than him.

He spent his days reading crime novels, his evenings watching television, and his weekends going out.

He met a twenty-year-old Ghanaese singer.

He met a twenty-three-year-old American law student.

He met a seventeen-year-old Sri Lankan au pair.

He met a thirty-five-year-old Brazilian dentist and a twenty-nine-year-old Dutch artist.

He met a fifteen-year-old Italian school girl.

He didn't mention any of this to his lover.

Half a year later he ran into a sixteen-year-old girl at a nightclub who told him her mother was Danish and her father Canadian.

They began a relationship that lasted seven months.

Just a few hours after the businesswoman rushed back to her office, the girl would turn up in her school uniform.

When one day she played hooky from school, mother and daughter ran into each other on the stairs.

That same evening, two body-builder types arrived at his door.

He spent three days at the hospital, and when he was released, he didn't have a place to live.

He slept at a twenty-four-year-old Lithuanian girl's place for a month, and when his face had healed, she encouraged him to apply to the escort service that she worked for.

After a few jobs the boss pulled him to the side.

—You're a natural, she said.

In no time he got a number of steady, very generous clients.

—You're more Keanu Reeves than Keanu Reeves, one of them said.

He bought the flat in which he still lives, and two years later a black Porsche.

He bought some of his furniture at a young antique dealer's shop just around the corner on Portobello Road, and over time the two have become friends.

Now and then they go out and play snooker.

Now and then they go to a pub and watch soccer.

Sometimes he lends him his car when he and his girlfriend go on a golf retreat for a weekend.

He hasn't told them how he makes his living.

He doesn't think it's anyone's business.

He needs to protect his clients.

He works out three times a week in a fitness center on Lillie Road.

He doesn't pop pills.

He eats only organic food.

He has begun to study Economics at the University of London.

At the bookstore across the street, two young blokes work on the weekend.

Several times he has heard them blasting Robbie Williams' version of George Michael's "Freedom."

Half-concealed by his Designer's Guild curtains, he watches them.

They dance.

They open boxes and shelve books and dance.

He hasn't talked to his family in nine years, and when he was contacted by a Danish anthropologist who was working on a series of articles about expat Danes, he didn't respond.

He recalled a TV series called "Lost Danes," and pictured a teary-eyed reunification accompanied by pan flute music.

When a second request arrived, he googled the man's name and discovered that he'd attended university with one of his friends.

It was the same friend who one night at Konrad said:

—Your problem is that you get too much pussy.

He'd smiled in response, and a bloke who'd stood beside them had turned and said:

—I wish I had that kind of problem.

A few days later he ended up responding anyway.

He would participate on the condition that they did not use his real name.

What irritates her most about Americans is their eloquence.

An American can sell anything, anytime.

It's something they learn in school.

From the first grade on, her girls have been asked to stand in front of their class and talk about their favorite toy.

When they whine for something new, they already sound like tiny salespeople.

—It's so awesome, says the youngest. It can sing and dance. It can't do everything, but pretty close.

Show and tell, she thinks.

When she watches an actor discuss his new film on David Letterman, or when George W. Bush gives his

State of the Union Address, or when the commercials come on: Show and tell.

Her husband is the manager of an elevator company.

They live on Boston Boulevard, in the Boston-Edison district, not far from the house where Henry Ford once lived.

They have three cars and two Jacuzzis: one on the terrace and one in the upstairs bathroom.

They have a swimming pool.

They have a gardener and a maid, both Black, or African American as she has learned to say.

They're not as diligent as the ones they had in Jakarta, but the good thing is that they're not Muslims.

She herself has a business degree and considers herself a Christian.

She tries to maintain the Danish traditions.

They have evening prayers, for example, and sing Danish songs.

Things they never did back home.

She has a girlfriend who is a theologian and works in marketing.

Every once in a while she thinks of their nights out when they lived in Aarhus.

She recalls the time they fell into conversation with the controversial developer Kurt Thorsen.

She recalls the time they met one of the guys from the band Fielfraz.

Her girlfriend went with him to the restroom and

returned twenty minutes later and took a giant swig of her beer.

Today she's married to an office head and has three children.

She hasn't seen her in a year and a half.

She hasn't seen her parents in seven months.

She was interviewed by an anthropologist, however.

He wanted to hear about her relationship to Denmark.

—You don't notice it when you live there, she said. But when you're far away, then you discover that it actually means something.

The anthropologist explained that his work was part of a large research project, but that a number of the interviews were published in an abridged version in *Politiken*.

The female photographer snapped a bunch of pictures, both of her and their house.

The pair seemed a little awkward around each other.

Her husband is a professor in biochemistry, and she is a Ph.D. student at the Center for Evolutionary Genetics.

They live in the area of campus reserved for staff.

Some of the streets have Spanish names, Vista Bonita, Los Trancos Drive, but most are named after a writer or a scientist: Twain Street, Newton Court, etc.

One of them is named after Gregor Mendel, and if

there were to be a deeper meaning in any of this, then she would live there.

Apparently there isn't.

They live on Fuentes Street, and she rarely has time to read literary fiction.

Her husband grew up in East L.A. and has an English-sounding name even though his parents are Mexican Americans.

His mother grew up in Texas and hasn't been to Mexico in forty years.

—It's so filthy, she says whenever they discuss going down there. You who have such a lovely house. Why would you go there?

His father is a gardener—or landscaper as it's called here.

He takes care of rich people's lawns and is always very friendly to her.

When she sees sixteen-foot-tall trees being transported on the roads, she thinks of him.

Her husband has three brothers.

One is on crack, one is in the military, and one is a businessman.

All three have mustaches.

—Why don't you? she asked him one day.

—Then I never would've met someone like you, he said, smiling.

She had Lasik surgery at a clinic in Torrance shortly after she moved here.

Her hair swiftly grew blonder, her skin darker.

Suddenly she didn't mind what she saw in the mirror.

For the first time ever, she felt what it was like to be popular.

She briefly dated another Ph.D. student, a Greek man who, at an Indian restaurant in Laguna Beach, declared:

—You are so beautiful it makes me nervous!

Several times she had noticed a handsome black-haired man in a green corduroy jacket sitting alone and eating at B.C.'s Cavern on the Green.

One day in October he came over and asked if he could sit at her table.

They went to the movies and to dinner, and several weeks passed before he even tried to kiss her.

She liked the slowness.

There was less confusion that way.

On a weekend trip to Santa Catalina, they spent the night at a little hotel where there was a jacuzzi in the room, and there she saw him naked for the first time.

That was in the middle of December.

From then on things moved rather quickly, but that was also just right.

He proposed to her in April, and in September they were married in Hawaii.

The wedding took place on a beach, there was a breeze, and the ceremony was performed by a judge whose white comb-over stood right up and revealed a freckled dome.

Her parents, her siblings, and her three best friends traveled all the way from Denmark.

A few other Ph.D. students participated as well.

Her sister danced with his father.

Her father danced with his mother.

Her mother danced with the youngest brother who was clean for the occasion.

She was enraptured.

They had wreaths of flowers around their necks, the band wore silver-colored suits and sombreros.

It was the first time she saw all four brothers together, and she was amazed at how much they looked alike.

I am glad they dress so differently, she thought.

That same autumn they bought the house in University Hills.

They bought an extra car.

They did their jobs and took small trips: San Francisco, Yucatan, Santa Fe.

They fucked.

He wasn't Catholic, but modest enough to order their condoms online.

They arrived 50 rubbers at a time, in a discrete, very light package.

They never lasted more than a few months.

—You're ruining me, he said.

—Then maybe we shouldn't bother with them anymore, she blurted.

—Oh, well, he said and smiled.

She didn't know where that had come from.

They agreed not to have children until she finished her degree.

For Christmas they visited her parents in Silkeborg, Denmark, and to her horror, she rediscovered her awkward old self in the mirror at the end of the hallway.

Maybe it was because her graduation photo still hung in the kitchen, or because they slept in her old bedroom?

Or maybe it was because all the women ogled him?

There were girls on the pedestrian shopping street and older women too.

The woman next door invited them for port wine and cookies and showed photographs of her trip to Lanzarote, where she went around more or less naked.

—She's got a little problem, her father said afterward, raising an imaginary glass to his mouth.

It didn't seem to bother her husband.

—The Danes are very friendly people, he said.

They visited her childhood friend in Aarhus and met her new boyfriend, an anthropologist who'd recently separated from his wife.

He asked with interest what it was like to live in California.

Some months later she got an email from him.

He and her girlfriend had broken up in the meantime, and it was only after getting express permission that she replied.

In the middle of August, he showed up in a rental

car along with a thin, dark-haired female photographer whom she immediately decided not to mention.

It was with mixed emotions that she showed them around campus.

They visited the center where she did her research, and later also Laguna Beach and Crystal Cove.

She told them how stupid she'd felt to begin with.

She told them about the time she needed cinnamon and had forgotten to look up the word before she went to the supermarket.

All the spices were sealed, so she had to take the long way home and look it up in her red dictionary.

Just the fact of not having a car!

She told them about how, after a few weeks, her kitchen sink had begun to smell.

The drain was just a big hole covered with rubber flaps, and not until a man from Maintenance arrived to examine it did she discover the garbage disposal. It was full of vegetable peels and that kind of thing.

She could go on and on in that vein.

The girl photographer didn't say that much, just walked around with her camera, like someone from a magazine, and suddenly she felt once again like the girl with eyeglasses and graduation cap.

She hadn't the slightest desire to introduce them to her husband, but of course on the way through Aldrich Park they ran into him.

He greeted them warmly and said something nice about Denmark.

The photographer looked a little skeptical, and she just hoped that her husband didn't notice.

She kissed his cheek and tugged them along at once.

That evening she whispered to him:

—Can we do it without?

Later, when they lay panting and she could feel his sperm oozing out of her, he said:

—Danish girls have got to be the most beautiful in the world.

She's training to become a diamond-cutter.

She rents a room from an elderly Belgian woman and is dating an Indian man from Gujarat.

She can't resist his soft d's.

She can't resist his big-eyed sincerity.

She can't resist his dark-brown cock: flaccid, it's nearly black.

They meet at hotels or, when the old woman isn't home, at her place.

His family runs a business on Hovenierstraat.

Her parents are Jews, but her affection for Jewish history or religion is limited.

She attended public school in Denmark and has Danish friends.

She's tired of hearing about the Holocaust.

She wasn't accepted into the Design Academy and then heard about the school here in Antwerp.

People come here from all around the globe.

They teach you how to cut the old-fashioned way.

Here they teach you about the four c's: cut, clarity, carat, and color, about the 57 or 58 cuts of the brilliant, about Buddha cut, czar cut, northern lights, and all the others.

There are synthetic diamonds and genuine.

There are irradiated and those that come from conflict zones in Africa.

She learns to use a computer: It calculates which cut renders the least waste.

She considers continuing her studies at De Beers School in Johannesburg.

She considers marrying her boyfriend.

He hasn't proposed, but she knows it's the only solution for them if they don't want to keep meeting in secret.

He would like to move to the USA.

She would like to be a jewelry artist.

When she hears about his family and the way they live, she thinks: I'll never do that.

Recently she was interviewed by a Danish anthropologist and photographed in the middle of the throng on Hovenierstraat.

The interview was published in a Danish newspaper and precipitated a number of emails from back home, among them one from an old boyfriend whom she in a weak moment invited for a visit.

He never took her up on it, but sometimes she thinks about that female photographer.

Sometimes she sits in the reading room at Museum Plantin-Moretus and thumbs through the old books.

She has found a dissertation from the 17th century on precious gems, and she has riffled through an old book called *Chroniques de Froissart*.

About halfway in there's an image of a handsome young soldier who is the spitting image of the photographer.

THREE

The fourth time I visit Varvara, she goes into her office and retrieves a sheet of paper.

—You want something about the famous people I've met, right? If we print this list, then that's covered. I even slept with a few of them.

Poul Reichhardt
Idi Amin
Michael Strunge
H.C. Hansen
Jens Otto Krag
Jens August Schade
Ole Olsen (the film director)
Otto Brandenburg
Otto Leisner
Otto B. Lindhardt
Cary Grant
King Christian X
King Frederik IX
Sophus Krølben
Ole Olsen (the speedway racer)
Ingmar Bergman
Kurt Thorsen

—Idi Amin? I say.

—Yes. He demanded we call him "Lord of all the beasts of the earth and fishes of the sea and conqueror of the British Empire."

Knirke calls from Stromboli.

She tells me about the writer they have interviewed.

He lives in a large white house with a view of the sea.

She tells me about the volcano that regularly sends clouds of smoke into the air, and about the hotel they live in: There's a swimming pool filled with saltwater, and a painter has decorated all the rooms.

—There are purple flowers on my headboard. It's one of those iron beds. You should see it.

—I would like to, I say.

—Mmm, she says.

I'm relieved that they have separate rooms.

She sends me the interview shortly afterward, and the next day it's published in *Politiken*.

It's accompanied by two of her photographs: One of the writer with the volcano as a backdrop and one of a strange, reddish-brown cliff towering over the sea.

I transcribe the tape and stare at the photo of the cliff. I can just make out some tiny figures hiking on it, and there's a little white lighthouse on its right side.

Johanne calls.

I listen to the message a short time later.

—I just wanted to know how you were doing?

Varvara had three children with Phil in the course of four years: William, Elizabeth, and Leonard. They looked like their father, and when she and Phil's younger sister Isabell went walking with them, people automatically assumed Isabell was the mother.

They lived in a 1,300-square foot villa and had a maid, a gardener, and two nannies.

When Varvara, seven months after Leonard's birth, wanted to resume her acting lessons, she and Phil clashed.

She didn't allow herself to be cowed, and a year later, when she completed her studies with distinction and was offered the role of Miss Julie at one of the big theatres, the result was a fresh round of arguments.

—My wife is *not* public domain! Phil shouted and slammed the door, raining plaster down.

Soon afterward, she found a recent rental receipt for the flat near the British Museum, a lease she thought had been terminated long ago, and in revenge she began having an affair with her counterpart Jean.

He was married and his name was Stanley Baker.

When Phil, foaming after the premiere, asked whether she'd slept with the waiter, she admitted it without hesitation.

He, however, proclaimed his innocence.

There was no proof, and when the authorities didn't find it likely that Varvara could provide for the children, she lost her parental rights in the divorce that followed.

Six years earlier, they had spent their honeymoon in Antibes, and on the third day there he'd stepped on a sea urchin. She spent an entire afternoon removing the spikes with pincers, and finally he said, Oh, well. Let's fuck.

When he suddenly died during a safari somewhere in Africa seven years after the divorce, doctors discovered a small spike wedged into the right chamber of his heart.

Johanne leaves a message:

—Wanna come over? I've made lentil soup.

I call Knirke.

She's stranded.

The wind is so strong the hydrofoil can't dock.

She tells me there's a small bookstore close to the hotel, with a courtyard and a gray-haired woman serving tea and biscotti.

She's sat there reading most of the day with a snoring cat perched on her lap.

—It made me think of you.

—Do I snore?

—Mmm. I don't mean the snoring.

—Have you two been up on the volcano?

—No, it's too windy.

Stanley Baker wasn't so happy about being dragged into Varvara's divorce.

He broke off their affair, and during the last fourteen shows he alternated between barking and hissing his lines at her.

The director was elated.

—That's just what I'd like to see: class resentment! Contempt!

—Call me, Johanne says on the answering machine.

I watch the blue house across the street. The television is on in one of the apartments. I can see a man rowing in a kayak. Below, an immigrant woman is vacuuming.

I call Johanne.

She doesn't pick up the telephone, and I leave a message:

—I just wanted to hear how you were doing.

Varvara acted alongside David Baron in Agatha Christie's *And Then There Were None*.

He suggested that they smoke marijuana.

—Tonight we'll swap lines, he said to her. That'll wake them up.

He was later known by his real name: Harold Pinter.

An email from Johanne arrives:

Subject: How I'm doing

Today I masturbated with a baby corn in memory of you.

I burned your books in the kitchen sink and regret

ever saying nice things about them.

I read Hélène Cixous and ate gummy bears and thought about how

you enjoyed humiliating me.

I never want to see you again.

I get a text message from Knirke:
i'm on my way
to London.

Varvara was granted custody after Phil's death, and a year later, when she was offered a part at The Royal Danish Theater, she and the children moved to an apartment on Duntzfelt's Allé in Hellerup.

Following the advice of a colleague, she approached Principal C.C. Kragh-Müller and signed her children up for the Bernadotte School.

William was eleven, Elizabeth nine, and Leonard eight.

None of them spoke Danish.

She hired a nanny and a private tutor.

The latter was a stooped, recent graduate from Hanstholm who kept strict discipline and began the day with a Thøger Larsen song or a poem by Johannes V. Jensen.

When the first of them was accepted at Hellerupvej, the others quickly followed suit.

Here they didn't sing morning songs.

Here there were no school uniforms, and William was teased for his tie.

He insisted on wearing it.

He refused to speak Danish.

He subscribed to the English hunting magazine *The Field* and started taking riding classes at the Ordrupdal Riding Club.

Leonard, on the other hand, let his hair grow out, wore checkered pants, and began to play bass guitar.

Elizabeth spent most of her time at the school's library, where she read novels by Tove Ditlevsen and Martin Andersen Nexø.

Varvara got favorable reviews for her first role as Esther in *Inside the Walls*, but she noticed the skepticism between the lines and in the dressing room.

—Well? Jørgen Reenberg said. Now what?

—If I sound funny, it's because I've got a contact high, Knirke says.

—What's that I can hear in the background?

—That's a playground. I've come to the park to get a little fresh air. We're staying at Mikael's cousin's place. They're up in the apartment smoking pot.

—And when is the interview?

—Tomorrow. I'm a bit nervous about it. He sounds strange. He's a professional escort, and we're not allowed to use his real name.

—I hope he's not too attractive.

—I've always been too cheap to pay for sex.

—Yeah, it would quickly add up. You're right.

—Mmm.

I wake to the telephone ringing. It's Andreas.

—Did I wake you? he asks.

—Oh, no.

—How are you doing? Won't you send me just a few pages, so I can see how it's moving along?

—Oh, sure. I'll send you something later today.

I get an email from Johanne:

Subject: Excrements

I'm going to Aarhus now to do a reading and return tomorrow evening.

I have put a bag with various things out in the hallway and I ask that you pick it up before I return—otherwise it will be thrown away.

The contents are:

A green T-shirt, unwashed

Three pairs of socks, unwashed

A pair of jeans, stained, unwashed

Ovid's *Metamorphosis*

A pack of Durex Thins with four remaining (I've used one)

A can of espresso, quarter full

A set of bicycle lights

Fuck you

PS: Please throw the key to my apartment through the letter slot.

The fifth time I visit Varvara, we drink vermouth starting at ten o'clock in the morning, and after an hour we switch to gin and tonics.

She's in a bad mood.

—Knud and I had a fight.

At two o'clock she sends me home.

—I need a nap, she says.

That same evening, I send ten pages to Andreas.

I get an email from Knirke. She writes that she might have a layover in Copenhagen on the way from Los Angeles to Antwerp. She asks that I reserve that day. She writes that she'd like to spend nine out of ten hours in my bed.

She attaches three photographs: One of a black Porsche, one of a bookstore called The Travel Bookshop, and one of herself.

She's dressed in a black T-shirt that reads "I miss you madly."

I pick up the bag with my things.

As I'm standing there, I remember my Gertrude Stein books.

I am just about to put the key in the lock but change my mind and throw it through the mail slot.

I call Sune.

—Would you like to get a beer? I'm just around the corner.

—I don't know, he says. It's not a good time right now. I'll call you one of these days.

I drink espresso and riffle through Ovid's *Metamorphosis*.

Varvara met her third husband in a men's room.

It was in the break between the first and second acts of *The Barber of Seville*.

Her bladder was about to burst, and there was a line to the ladies' room.

She discovered him only after she'd pulled down her nylon stockings.

The room was high-ceilinged.

The tank was positioned right under the stucco, and he'd clung to the pipe right where it angles out from the wall.

He scraped his feet against the tiles.

She couldn't hold it any longer and sat down to pee.

Then she helped him down.

She had to calm him first.

She stood on the toilet seat and stroked his shin.

—Sit down on my shoulders, she said.

He opened his eyes.

—Ooo, he said.

—It'll be all right, she said. I've tried it before.

That was a lie of course.

He scraped his feet, she poked, and finally he gave in.

Slowly he let his feet glide down from the tiles, and at once they hung dangling in the air.

Quickly he wrapped his legs around her neck.

She positioned her free hand on his thigh and then on his rump, and then one thing led to another.

He loosened his grip on her windpipe, and she hadn't quite predicted that he'd come to sit that way.

Neither of them returned to their seats.

That was in 1968.

He was German and had eaten mushrooms at The Deer Park in Jaegersborg.

His name was Lucan Katz.

—You shouldn't condense it so much, Andreas says.

I'm summoned to an urgent meeting in his office.

—You write really well, of course, but you've got to unpack the material a little more. This isn't a book for literary people. This is a book that will rest on coffee tables in small homes. We're talking 200 pages, minimum, *plus* a ton of pictures.

I'm sitting there looking up at his shelf and can't find my books. Two of Johannes' are up there despite the fact that Andreas isn't her editor.

—Eighty years divvied up in 200 pages. That's 2.5 years per page, just a rule of thumb. You develop her first forty years in ten pages. You see how that won't work, right?

—There's a lot going on right now.

—I've heard you two split up?

—That's right.

Neither of us say a word.

—It's never fun, that kind of thing, he says

—Not at all. And I've also begun to write something else. A novel, I think.

—Sounds cool, but maybe you can hold off on that for a while? We have to get Varvara's book started in six weeks if we're to keep on schedule. Maybe you need a little help? We could get someone to transcribe for you?

I nod.

—Yes, I say. That might be a good idea.

I sit staring at the photo of Knirke in the black T-shirt.

I call Sune, but he doesn't pick up.

—I thought it was time to have a pint, I say to the answering machine. How about eight o'clock down at the dive?

I glance at my watch. It's eight, which is to say that it's two o'clock in Detroit.

Knirke and I have agreed to send text messages and

emails instead of calling—because otherwise it will be too expensive.

She needs peace and quiet to sleep off her jetlag. Tomorrow they will interview some wealthy woman, and the day after that they fly to Los Angeles.

I get a hard-on at the thought that she's coming to Copenhagen in five days.

Lucan Katz wasn't just German: he was a poet.

The Goethe Institute had invited him to Copenhagen, and he was off to Iceland the very next day for a similar event.

He'd read alongside Per Højholt in the Writer's Union, among other things, and to Lucan's immense pleasure Højholt had inflated a balloon with a foot pump during his reading.

When Lucan visited Varvara on the way home from Reykjavik, they went to see the poet west of Silkeborg.

Varvara peeled potatoes on the terrace with his wife while the daughter ran around naked on the grass, and the two men walked in circles and strove to understand one another.

—We spent the night, and we never saw them again. But many years later he wrote a poem about us. I have it here somewhere.

She walks into the bedroom and returns with a small, yellowed chapbook that has a charcoal drawing on the cover.

I open up right to it:

Instead of writing a poem the poet *Lucan Katz* took
a shower. The poem he would have written instead
of a letter that couldn't, but had to, be a stand in for
his appearance at *Varvara Eng's*, his fiancée,
whom he hadn't seen in three weeks, but whom he
nonetheless loved so dearly that she had to leap
for her life so as not to become drenched.

I smile.

—It's pretty good, isn't it? Taking a shower wasn't his strong suit, but otherwise it's not off the mark. I've read all of Højholt's books because Lucan read them when he first learned Danish. I didn't understand a word, but they always made me horny. "Are you cheating on me with Per again?" Lucan would say whenever I sat with one of those strange chapbooks.

It's one in the morning, and I'm sitting there staring at a photo of a swimming pool Knirke sent me.

A Black man is cleaning it with a very long thingamajig.

A girl in a pink bathing suit is standing on the other side of the water.

She's pouting.

The wealthy may have it all, writes Knirke, but they are bored.

70

The next day I deliver the tapes from the first four interviews to the publisher. I keep the fifth, so I have something to work on in the meantime.

—Oh yes, Varvara says. Lucan was a terrific man, not even William could completely hate him. After a few months he moved in with us on Duntzfelt's Allé, and that same autumn we were married at Gentofte Town Hall. He was a fanatical atheist. Churches and especially priests gave him a strong case of the willies. He'd grow pale and get a stomach ache. It was actually rather sweet. We honeymooned in Rome and didn't see a single church, with the exception of the Pantheon which he loved for the hole in the ceiling. We met an Italian writer, as beautiful as a goddess, naturally, and very charmed by Lucan, and I became terribly jealous. So he brought me back to the hotel and cured me in the simplest possible way. We lived together for six years before he suddenly died of a heart attack, forty-seven years old. It was on a reading tour in Germany. There were twenty poets in a bus. To cope, he was constantly drunk. He was a funny man, but also vulnerable. He just didn't know it himself. There's so much men don't know about themselves, isn't there?

I try getting in touch with Sune, but he doesn't answer the phone.

I run into one of Johanne's girlfriends on the street, and she pretends she doesn't see me.

I get an email from Knirke:

It's beautiful here (we're staying right beside the Pacific Ocean), but I'm having a hard time concentrating. They have these huge trucks here that drive around with large advertising signs in the back. They don't do anything else. Isn't that crazy? See you in less than 30 hours!

The sixth time I visit Varvara, she's in a better mood.

—We've reconciled. It was something about his daughter, Emma's mother. I stepped on her toes. I invited her to lunch at Saison, and then we went to her place and drank tea. I apologized and apologized. I don't usually do that. But she's so terribly sweet, and I can't live without Knud.

We're sitting on the terrace, high up.

We're eating strawberries and drinking white wine.

—What about your Knirke? she suddenly asks. I see her photographs in the newspaper all the time. She is very talented. Will she be home soon?

The pickers are wearing big white hats and are scattered around the field.

When I pass them, they look up.

I recognize some of the faces: My mother, a girl I was in love with in fourth grade, my first girlfriend, a girl from high school, Johanne.

Knirke is walking farther ahead, and even though I pick up the pace, the distance between us remains the same.

The field is vast.

The strawberry scent is intense.

The sun shines, and all of the sudden Knirke is standing right beside me.

—Have you tasted them? she asks and shows me her breasts.

In place of nipples there are two strawberries.

—Aren't they funny?

Lucan's first wife and their twin sons showed up at his funeral.

The wife looked like something out a Fassbinder film with her bleached hair and her thick black eyeliner.

His sons were in their early twenties, and both had long hair. One of them wore military pants and a red shirt, the other wore a purple velvet suit.

They were very thin.

A German literature professor gave a long and unintelligible speech.

A Swedish colleague shouted a poem:

LUCAN!
LONGING!
LAWBREAKER!
LARK!
LAZY FUCK!

LUDICROUS!
LUGUBRIOUS!
LIFELESS!
LID!

Varvara cried, Elizabeth cried, and Trutti, his first wife, cried.

One of the sons began to bark like a dog.

Lucan was buried under an elm tree at Mariebjerg Cemetery.

Varvara knew that he didn't like cremations.

—I've partied my entire life. Let me be a party for worms!

Knirke sends a photo of a truck with a large advertisement on its bed. There's a silver-colored car, and in big letters it reads:

TOYOTA MOVING FORWARD.

She also sends one of the blond Ph.D. student they've interviewed.

She has a slightly startled look in her eyes and is standing in front of a white building.

I get an email from Johanne.

Subject: Pelle the Conqueror see Pelle No-Tail.

I thought you would return my things since you were coming by, but you apparently don't have that much empathy.

Here's my list:

My yellow summer dress

Chai

Jasmine tea

Overnight pads

Various CDs

Possibly other things

Put them at my door tomorrow evening

Fuck you

P.S. Sune is excellent at eating pussy

I leave a message on Sune's answering machine.

—It's okay. I know, and it's okay. Call me, okay?

Varvara played Christine in *Mourning Becomes Elektra* the same winter and had to face that wickedness became her.

The reviews praised her acting, and though it was the breakthrough she'd waited for, she was unable to enjoy it.

There was a certain satisfaction in the role, maybe because it allowed her to rage, but when she wasn't on the stage, she was so apathetic and distant that her children stopped calling her.

William was at agriculture school, Elizabeth studied literature, and Leonard toured the world with Savage Rose.

She forgot her own birthday in January and was first reminded of it when Elizabeth called late in the afternoon.

Elizabeth had her admitted to the psych ward at Gentofte that very evening.

I set the bag next to Johannes' door and am already by the stairwell when I hear a creaky floorboard inside the apartment.

I glance at the peep hole and can't see anyone.

I get a letter from my bank.

There's an overdraft of 19,432.77 kroner from my account, and they've blocked my debit card, effective immediately.

At the psychiatric ward they discovered Varvara was pregnant.

They ceased her medication and began intensive talk therapy.

—I think it saved me. Suddenly I could differentiate between what was normal pregnancy hysteria, and what was grief. It might sound banal but having a kind of order in the chaos made the madness lessen at once. Does it sound completely ridiculous?

—Makes sense to me, I say.

—I was forty-six and hadn't planned on having more children at all, but Cille is one of the best things to have happened in my life. I believe she was conceived the very last time Lucan and I were together. I remember how we lay on the sofa in the living room. We hadn't much time, and we didn't have any more condoms. "Be careful," I said. Well, he wasn't.

Knirke has asked me not to pick her up at the airport. Let's not waste time on that.

I've changed the bed sheets and cleaned the apartment. I've filled the fridge with food, spending money I borrowed from my sister.

I've bought a bottle of champagne and two bottles of wine and shoved books and magazines aside and put a few back again, so that it doesn't appear too tidy.

I've taken a shower.

She arrives ten minutes earlier than expected, and I've been ready for over an hour.

I'm a little sweaty.

Her lips seem at first strange and then familiar and soft.

—Are you hungry? I ask.

—Mmm, she says and begins to unbutton my shirt.

It's freshly ironed. I can't recall when I last ironed a shirt. She throws it on the floor.

I put my hand up under her blouse.

She's even more suntanned, I briefly note.

My telephone rings, and I don't bother answering.

My cell phone rings a moment later.

—You can answer it, Knirke says.

—It can wait, I say.

Knirke has put my ironing board across my bed, and we're sitting on either side eating with a pair of chopsticks.

We're eating Vietnamese.

We're drinking champagne.

—It tastes delicious, she says.

—Mmm, I say.

I'm so hungry that I'm trembling a little.

I feel drunk already after a single glass.

My belly is rumbling.

Knirke smiles.

—You get air in your belly with all that kissing. Just let me know if you want me to squeeze it.

—It's at your own risk.

—I'm not prissy, she says. Remember, I have three brothers.

We're sitting in a taxi on the way to the airport.

Knirke stares at the tall buildings in Ørestad, and I follow her gaze.

—I'll try to come home as soon as I can, she says.

—That would be lovely.

We say nothing more until we're standing in the departure hall.

After I've kissed her goodbye and watched her pick up her camera bag from the security belt, I take the train home.

I get an email from Andreas:

I tried to call. We have to talk as soon as possible.

I sleep nonstop for fourteen hours and wake when the telephone rings.

—Were you sleeping? Andreas says.

—No.

—Are you busy this afternoon?

An elderly woman with purple glasses is sitting in his office when I arrive.

—Gunilla, she says.

—Pelle.

Andreas says:

—Gunilla has listened to your tapes, and she would like to help. She has written a few actor biographies already.

—Okay?

—That will impact your fee, of course, but if this project is going to go anywhere, we need to change saddles as quickly as possible. What do you say?

—Um, yeah. Can I think it over?

—Of course. But preferably not too long. What we're noticing is that you spent a lot of time on an obscure German poet and forget people like Poul Reichhardt, Jens Otto Krag, and Ingmar Bergman.

After her breakthrough, Varvara started to get

inquiries from people she hadn't heard from in years. Countess Danneskiold, whom she'd played with as a child, invited her to her fiftieth birthday party, and the count from Langeland who'd once sent her roses and was now well into his eighties began to send small letters on handmade pink paper. At the height of her pregnancy she went to the countess's birthday party, but the reception she got there was more polite than warm. During the dinner, when she liberated her swollen feet from her recently purchased purple pumps, she aroused mild indignation.

I read the account of Pyramus and Thisbe in Ovid's *Metamorphosis*.

At two a.m. I send an email to Knirke:

Subject: P & T
Do you know the story of Pyramus and Thisbe? They arranged a secret rendezvous beside a mulberry tree. They didn't fare so well. There was a problem with a lion. Communication broke down. So they died. I will read it to you one day. Imagine if they'd had cellphones! I'm having trouble sleeping.

Knirke and Mikael are in Antwerp interviewing a Danish girl Knud knows there.

The next day I get photographs in an email.

There's an image of a black-haired girl in Jesus sandals crossing a busy street.

There's an image of a pink diamond.

There's an image of a Sikh man on his way out of a bank.

I got a little worried about the Pyramus and Thisbe email, Knirke writes. Are you okay?

I open the fridge and quickly close it again.

I glance in the cupboard and find some oats and a little spaghetti.

I eat toasted oats and consider whether I should ask my father for money.

We haven't spoken in a year and a half.

From my perspective, it would be quite all right if a few more years pass.

I consider contacting Knud.

I get three pages with probing questions from Gunilla.

I get another reminder from my unemployment office.

I get a reminder for rent and one from the phone company. My last telephone bill, which comes to 1,276,39 kroner including tax, should've been paid ten days ago.

I ask Andreas if I can get an extra advance, and I am told that I should rather pay money back.

—Can you leave tomorrow? Knud says.

Cille resembled her father.

She had coal-black hair and blue-gray eyes.

She was a colicky baby the first four and a half months of her life.

Every night from five to nine she screamed.

—When Cille began going to daycare, I began taking tai-chi classes and naps. I took a lover named Roger who was on staff at the American Embassy. He let himself in, and sometimes I woke up when he crawled into bed beside me. But when he began to ask me about my friends, I threw him to the curb. That was in the 1970s, after all. Everyone was so lefty back then. What a snake!

I'm sitting in an Air France plane, listening to Varvara's voice.

I have a Fjällräven money belt around my waist that Knud gave me.

There's a small, lined envelope in it which I'm not allowed to open.

FOUR

He has never been sociable in the morning, and now that he's stopped smoking, it's only grown worse.

He eats breakfast alone on the terrace with a view of the sea, while his wife potters around inside.

She figured it out long ago.

He has lived in Spain for nearly forty years, and she has lived here for fifteen.

She is Brazilian and a singer.

She has performed at a number of bars and nightclubs from La Linea to Nerja.

It's only been a few years since she retired.

He himself owned a bar and, before that, tried to make a go as a real estate agent, guide, and encyclopedia salesman.

That last was back home in Denmark.

Now he has written his memoir.

It begins at Bakken amusement park when his mother goes into the bushes with her boyfriend's friend and ends in Rincón de la Victoria the day they move into the house.

He hasn't managed to sell the memoir to a publisher, so he's printed fifty copies instead and shared them with friends and acquaintances.

From page 234 to 299, his wife writes about her life, and how they met.

She has found an attractive, cursive font on the computer and made it pink.

She is not the most beautiful woman he has seen, but the most beautiful he has slept with.

They drink a bottle of wine every night, but no more.

They have stopped going to the bars.

He has had skin cancer and gets a check-up every three months.

She's in good health.

She has a son who lives in Rio, and he has a daughter he never sees.

As far as he knows, she lives on the island of Møn, in Denmark.

She's a member of a cult.

It's a complicated story, and it's not included in his memoir.

They rarely get visitors, but now and then two Danish Jehovah's Witnesses stop by.

They are always very well dressed, and he rejects them with as much kindness as he is able.

Recently, an anthropologist and a photographer paid them a visit.

They came a little too early, and he had only just finished shaving.

He tried to hide his irritation, but it didn't help that the guy looked like someone who'd never held a job.

The girl took a raft of photos, first of just him, then together with his wife and finally only of her.

That was okay.

He pulled himself together, but then he thought about the time C.V. Jørgensen had a hit song in Denmark, in which "Costa del Sol" rhymed with "neo-Nazi and alcohol."

That summer a Danish journalist had entered his bar in Fuengirola and had begun to ask questions.

Soon someone shouted.

Soon someone wanted to give the journalist a good beating.

That was in the early '80s, but one would've thought it was in the self-righteous '70s.

What's wrong with a little partying, with enjoying life?

It all ended with a police report and a two-page spread in *Ekstra Bladet*, including a photo of him and several of his guests.

The image was developed in a way that made him look like a boiled lobster.

That's why he was a little on guard when he was interviewed.

That's why he was maybe a little snappish.

It's not the kind of thing he misses when, on rare occasions, he misses his homeland.

She has a weakness for news from small, out-of-the-way places.

Recently she watched a story on Reuter's homepage about some eight-million-year-old cypress trees that were found in an open lignite mine somewhere in Hungary.

The place was called Bukkabrany.

She couldn't convince her editor back home to run a feature on it.

The trees had stood in a thick layer of sand, were 13-20 feet tall, and not petrified.

They had a kind of conical shape.

Seeing the photos, she felt a diffuse longing or melancholy or joy, she couldn't tell which.

She knew better than to share these kinds of feelings with her husband or her colleagues, so she saved the images on her computer and looked at them periodically.

Some weeks later she met a Hungarian diplomat at a reception at the Jüdisches Museum and asked him what he knew about Bukkabrany.

He'd never heard of the place.

She told him about the cypresses, and he said:

—Oh, Bükkábrány. Yes, very interesting.

A few days later she got an invitation from the embassy: If she was interested in visiting the mine, they would make the necessary arrangements.

She accepted without consulting her boss.

She was seated at the gate and reading the *Frankfurter Allgemeine* when the diplomat showed up.

—Are you going home for a visit?

—I thought you might need a little assistance?

She smiled.

He was a little shy, but no more than what was becoming for a diplomat.

—That's very kind of you, she said.

He booked rooms for them at a small, four-star hotel around twenty-five miles from the mine.

He made sure they had a car, a cameraman, and interview appointments with relevant archaeologists.

One of them said:

—What's special about the trees is that they're not petrified or transformed into lignite. They've maintained their original structure. All because of a sandstorm eight million years ago. By studying their tree rings, we can now get a picture of the climate at that time.

It was clear that he'd repeated this information twenty or thirty times, but it was all right.

To stand 180 feet beneath the surface of the earth, between the thick tree trunks, was something in itself.

Possibly, it wasn't sufficient for television viewers; they would want information, interviews, etc., but for her it was enough.

The diplomat convinced her to stay an extra day and showed her various attractions in the area.

They ate grilled goose liver and drank apricot brandy, and she deftly avoided conversation topics or situations that could lead to greater intimacy than was appropriate.

He was pleasant company, but no more than that.

She had never been to Hungary.

In the afternoon on the final day, a Danish anthropologist called her up.

—Did you forget our appointment?

She apologized and they agreed to meet the following day.

Already in the airport she knew there would be problems.

Her travel partner suddenly grew quiet.

On the plane she pretended she was asleep.

Not until they stood at the baggage carrousel did they materialize:

—This has been an exquisite pleasure, he said, clasping her right hand between each of his.

Was that a tiny tear in the corner of his eye?

What did she actually know about him?

Did he have a wife, children at home?

She thanked him for all his help and hurried away with her wheeled suitcase.

The following morning, she received a bouquet.

Her husband, who'd met her with greater warmth than she was accustomed to, made a pained face, but said nothing.

During the interview that same afternoon, she kept

seeing the tall, slightly over-polite man in her mind.

She spoke of Berlin, of the many changes the city had undergone in just a few years, of its greatness, its history, its charming artist districts in the old East Berlin, and the entire time she thought of the diplomat and his flowers.

The next morning another bouquet arrived, and her husband left without saying goodbye.

She edited the feature on her computer and sent it to the news desk.

Use it or not, she wrote. It hasn't cost the station a dime.

—Listen, she told her husband that evening. He's a diplomat and went along on the trip. He helped me with all the practical matters. Absolutely nothing happened. He means nothing to me.

The bouquets continued to arrive, and after the seventh she called him.

—You have to stop this, she said. It doesn't make any sense. You're complicating my life.

—My apologies, he replied. I'm so sorry.

He ended the call almost at once.

To her own surprise, she was a little disappointed.

They live in a five-room apartment in the middle of Jakriborg.

The house they live in is brand new but built in the style of an old Hanseatic house with a tall gable facing the street.

The street is laid with cobblestones, and there are black street lights made of wrought iron and glass.

The houses are all different.

They have timber frames, dormer and bay windows and are painted in a plethora of colors.

There's a city wall.

The children roam freely and have already made a lot of friends.

They go to Swedish school, but also take classes in Danish.

He commutes to Kastrup where he works in passport control, and she's gotten a job in a daycare center close by.

—Just because it's new doesn't make it good, she says to him, and he says:

—I feel as good as new, though.

They discuss having an afterthought child and about limiting their carbon emissions.

They've been interviewed in *Politiken* by an anthropologist, and they told him how much they like the city. They showed him and a photographer around.

They weren't cited incorrectly, but the headline was a little pointed: "Bourgeois Christiana."

It was something the man had asked about:

—Is Jakriborg the bourgeois answer to Christiana?

—I've never been to Christiana, her husband had replied, and she'd said:

—There certainly aren't any biker gangs here. Or immigrant gangs. I would never let my children out of my sight in Christiana. Would you?

They've bought a telescope and registered for a class in Lund.

They've been to Kivik and bought unfiltered apple juice and fresh fish at the harbor.

They've been to Vimmerby to visit Astrid Lindgren's World.

There were miniature editions of Katholt, Bullerby, and Villakulla. There was a real-life Emil and a Pippi.

Through their youngest they have become good friends with a Danish-Swedish couple.

He's a wine salesman and she's a chef at a restaurant in Malmö.

They also live in Jakriborg.

—Don't make too much of it, said the chef the second time they visited.

They had slaved in the kitchen most of the day.

—I like a quite ordinary dinner. You don't need foam and *fois gras* and raw, marinated meat. I eat those things every day. I hope it doesn't sound ungrateful, but I would rather my profession weren't a hindrance. People hardly dare to cook for me anymore!

He is 57 and a former CEO.

He has always had a soft spot for Monty Python.

After three drinks, he sometimes begins to sing "Always Look on the Bright Side of Life," and after three more: "Lumberjack Song."

When he was fired in 2005, he and his wife moved to Torquay, in southern England.

The climate was pleasant, the neighbors friendly. But then, on an extended weekend in Scotland, they played at the Moray Golf Club course in Lossiemouth, and they saw a small hotel nearby for sale.

His wife found it afterwards on the Internet, and for a few weeks they looked at the images several times a day.

There were twelve rooms, a cozy library with a hearth and leather chairs, a bar, a dining hall, and a view of the bay.

There was a lovely little apartment for the owners.

He began calling his wife Sybil after the wife in *Fawlty Towers*:

—Well, Sybil, fancy buying a nice little hotel?

They drove up there again and were shown around by a young real estate agent with a large gap between his front teeth.

They spent five days in the area and stayed at a new hotel every night to study the competition a little.

He contacted an acquaintance in the travel industry back home in Copenhagen and inquired into the market for golf trips.

They put a third of his golden handshake on the table and sold the house in Torquay.

They spent more than three million kroner renovating and painting and opened the following spring.

He sent brochures to his old club in Hørsholm and to old friends and business connections.

With help from their son-in-law they built a website.

For the first few months, things were quiet, but after a few articles were published in *Børsen* and *Berlingske Tidende,* business began to pick up.

Suddenly they were booked several weeks in advance.

Suddenly his wife couldn't keep up.

They hired one of the locals to clean and make the beds, and he handled reception himself, arranged trips, gave good advice about golf courses and distilleries, and served breakfast and dinner.

He also tended the bar.

He'd never been so busy.

For the first time since he'd worked as a chauffeur one summer when he was quite young, he did manual labor.

It was much different than the team leader meetings and lunches and conferences and Board seminars he had spent his adult life doing.

The exhaustion he felt when he put his head to his pillow at night was something else.

He felt satisfied.

He had no concerns.

They chatted with guests and called each other Basil and Sybil.

—Where is Manuel when you really need him? he might say.

That first summer they had a guest who was a former boss for a company he owed a large sum of money to (a failed business venture in the early '80s), and he lost a few nights' sleep.

Over a Glenmoray one late night, however, the man told him that he'd been fucked over by the Board.

They played a round of golf in Lossiemouth the following morning, and he purposefully hit his ball in the bunker.

The man was now a loyal customer and came several times a year and got a nice discount on his room.

In September 2008, one of their son's friends visited.

He was an anthropologist and was traveling around with a female photographer.

They each got their own room.

When the woman wasn't busy with her camera, she seemed oddly distant.

She went to bed early.

The anthropologist seemed happy and contented as long as she was close by.

Late one evening he confided to them that he was getting a divorce.

There were two children involved, a girl of three and a boy of seven.

🌍

When he thinks about his childhood, he thinks about cheap brown toilet paper that doesn't absorb a thing.

He lives with his family in the Dubai suburb of Jumeira, and from the first floor they can see Burj al Arab, the world's only seven-star hotel.

He's employed at Executive Air, an English company with offices in Africa, the Middle East, and Asia.

In a Gulfstream G150 or G550 he flies businessmen and women to meetings or the jet set to vacations anywhere around the globe.

He grew up in a commune just outside of Holbæk.

His wife is a nurse, but she hasn't worked in five years.

They wouldn't dream of moving back home, but if they'd had the money, they would have bought the 463,000 square foot artificial island named Denmark in the prestigious local project The World.

Their two children go to an American school just around the corner, and the eldest of the two has a friend from the Emirates.

Otherwise, they spend most of their time with expats.

They meet at the golf club or at private dinners.

As non-Muslims, it's easy to purchase alcohol for

consumption at home, but you have to apply for a license.

The hangovers are ten times worse here because of the heat, so he tries not to drink as much.

Both his parents are alcoholics of the red wine generation.

They divorced in 1980 and both quickly found a new partner.

Neither was any happier, but they both became quite clearly poorer.

He can't stand his father's manner (he's a high school teacher, English and History), but he keeps in touch with him for the children's sake.

His mother lives with another woman.

—I have four grandmothers, he has heard his daughter tell one of her friends.

The very sight of his father and his wife in the airport, with their second-hand clothes and their sandals, makes his palms sweat.

When his mother and her girlfriend come to visit, he sends his wife to pick them up.

The friend is a reflexologist and a clairvoyant and a crystal healer and smiles indulgently no matter what he says or does.

After two days he's ready to explode.

In September, they had a visit from a photographer and an anthropologist.

He let his wife entertain them and only agreed to be interviewed.

When the anthropologist told them that they were heading to China, he couldn't keep his mouth shut.

He explained how he'd begun to learn Chinese.

He told them all the swear words that he'd learned:

"Tā māde niǎo" means "his mother's dick."

"Cào nǐ zǔzōng shíbā dài" means "fuck your forefathers eighteen generations back."

He told them about a Chinese tradition he'd read about: gambling on crickets.

It's almost like cockfighting.

It's illegal, of course, but nevertheless very popular.

He also told them that Executive Air has applied for clearance to open a division in Shanghai, and that they'd indicated he would have a top position.

He called the anthropologist that same evening and asked him to remove that part.

—No problem, he said. I'll erase it right away.

They haven't said anything to the kids yet.

They love Dubai.

In Burj al Arab there's an underwater restaurant.

In Dubai Emirates Mall there's an indoor ski slope 1,200 feet long.

In Wild Wadi Water Park there's an aquatic roller coaster that goes up to fifty miles per hour.

He has worked at Danida for four years.

He's a biologist and helps the local administration preserve the country's great wetlands.

On his travels around the country, he drives a dented red Toyota Land Cruiser.

One of the dents was caused by a gnu that got a bloody beard but survived thanks to a local veterinarian.

Now and then he brings his girlfriend along, a Black twenty-five-year-old teacher.

They have been to Zanzibar, and on the beach they saw a Portuguese man o' war the size of a human washed up on the shore.

She told him of a friend who had fainted in pain when he swam into one.

His girlfriend had saved him from the water at the last moment.

Since then, they've read on the Internet that a Portuguese man o' war isn't one animal, but four different colonies of small polyps that work closely together.

He himself is part Bornholmer, and she is part Maasai.

She works at a school in a poor suburb where there are more than forty kids in each classroom, and where a third of the parents are illiterate.

A quarter of them have AIDS.

He admires her engagement.

He's four inches taller than her, but her legs are much longer than his.

They have both been tested for HIV by his doctor.

He would like a house in a nice suburb and maybe a couple of children, but right now he's got his hands full.

Lake Victoria, Lake Malawi, and Lake Tanganyika: 20,000 square miles of Tanzania is covered by water.

Recently, he was interviewed by an anthropologist and the interview was published in *Politiken*.

His mother was excited.

—And what a lovely photo! she said. With the giraffes and your girlfriend.

The female photographer and his girlfriend got along really well.

They went out to see her school.

The photographer took a ton of shots of the children as they did gymnastics in the playground.

That evening the four of them went out dancing.

The men flocked around the photographer, and the anthropologist seemed uncomfortable.

She, though, took it in stride.

She told them to visit her if they ever came to Denmark.

She is an artist and has exhibited her work around the globe.

She is listed in Weilbach.

She puts stuff in boxes and seals them with a window pane.

It might be a photo of a whale and a defective hairdryer, a Turkish tea glass and a beautiful old chair, thirty cans of Spam and a thimble made of silver.

The American artist Joseph Cornell is one of her sources of inspiration.

She and her husband have lived in China for three years.

He is Dutch and runs a large brewery.

A few weeks after the Olympics, she got a visit from a Danish anthropologist and his female photographer.

They wandered around The Forbidden City together, and the anthropologist asked her about being a Dane in China.

Did she feel diminished because she couldn't express herself in Danish in her everyday life?

Did she see her art in a Danish or an international connection?

The young photographer stayed in the background a bit.

When the interview was winding down, the anthropologist asked if she, by any chance, knew anything about the Chinese and their relationship to crickets.

—Not so much, she said. I've seen the booths at the market, and I've heard there are some illegal gambling dens here and there. Why?

—I've just found out about it recently. Someone told me there were people who doped their crickets with Ecstasy.

He kept talking about them.

He wanted to visit a real gambling den.

—I don't think that's a good idea, she said. As far as I know, the authorities have begun to crack down on that.

He pressed until she finally called a friend who was more familiar with the shadier sides of the city's nightlife.

To tease the anthropologist, she took them down to Guo Li Zhang afterward.

Usually she can't get her husband or his male friends to go there.

They serve dick.

You can choose between ram, bull, donkey, dog, horse, deer, yak, snake, and seal.

They are usually grilled.

—As an anthropologist, the man said, one should be willing to try anything.

He ordered yak.

The photographer ordered deer and ate the slender, tenderloin-like piece of meat with a somewhat cautious expression on her face.

Five

Varvara was taking a nap when the telephone rang one day in the late '70s.

Cliff had been found naked at the bottom of the manure tank.

A few days later, one of the foresters was arrested and charged with manslaughter.

During the trial, it was revealed that he'd had a relationship with Cliff for many years.

Some weeks before, he'd been jilted for a soccer referee who was a math teacher at one of the county's schools.

The forester was 6'5 and cried during his confession.

The soccer referee seemed unaffected.

Cliff's wife, Benedikte, suddenly needed an estate manager.

She gave notice to the commune that had rented the tenant farm, and let William and his English wife, a riding master by the name of Abigail, move in.

William had just completed his studies at the agricultural college.

He bought his first Land Rover and a pair of knickerbockers.

They established a stud farm.

Upon arrival in the Ivory Coast, I am pulled aside by a customs official.

He offers to organize the necessary papers for a fee of 50 American dollars.

I begin to sweat.

Knud has told me it is a common practice, so I quickly pay.

When I get outside, it's dark, and I take a taxi to the hotel.

The driver speaks French, and I don't understand that much.

He speaks almost nonstop during the half-hour ride.

The hotel is called Résidence Isabelle and is pink.

My room is actually two rooms: a suite with Internet, air conditioning, and a view of the lagoon.

I take a cold shower.

I get a text from Knirke:

be careful,
okay?

The receptionist has arranged a car and driver for me, and at 9:00 a.m. the following morning we drive north in a white Jeep.

It's humid and over ninety degrees outside, but in the car it's cool and comfortable.

The driver's name is Mamadou, and he knows a few words of English.

We drive on a wide, four-lane highway through the jungle.

In a clearing I see a man with two oxen and a wooden plow. He's wearing a red baseball hat.

We pass a mud building with sharp, pyramid-shaped towers of varying heights.

We pass a truck with twenty or twenty-five children on the flatbed. Several have a white rash on their faces.

We meet a convoy of UN soldiers.

We're still surrounded by jungle when the driver points.
—*C'est la. La plus grande du monde.*
I spot a gray-white cupola with a gold cross on top.
I haven't had time to buy guide books or read up on the Internet. All I have is a slip of paper with a name: Basilique de Notre Dame de la Paix in Yamoussoukro.
As we approach, I come to think of a TV feature I saw many years earlier.

Two curved colonnades surround the oblong common like an octopus's tentacles.
In the middle of the common is a mosaic that depicts a gigantic white dove.

I walk over to it, up the stairs, and through the tall doors.

Knud has said that I should seat myself somewhere visible in the center of the church, so I sit down underneath the cupola, on one of the many pews made of a solid dark wood.

I lay the lined envelope down on my right.

After around ten minutes, a Black monk sits down beside me.

He wears a dark-gray cloak with a small cowl.

He begins to pray.

I study a glass mosaic depicting Jesus and the twelve apostles.

Jesus is riding a sheep, and beneath him a Black man raises his hands into the air.

Their hoods are more or less the same color.

I notice the bench creaking faintly and I discover that the monk is leaving.

Beside me now is another, slightly larger envelope.

I have been told not to open it.

Mamadou drives me directly to the airport.

Two young poets, Michael Strunge and Henrik S. Holck, paid Varvara a visit. They wanted to hear about Lucan.

They invited her to some readings.

After she heard F.P. Jac for the first time, she went up to him.

—That was so wonderful, she said, and the poet thanked her shyly.

She chatted with Poul Borum.

—He was so sweet. I remember that he wore leopard-skin pants and studded leather bracelets. He liked to stick his tongue out.

At a fundraiser for the magazine *Sidestreet* she read some of Lucan's poems.

She stopped napping and dyed her hair red.

She began having an affair with a director fifteen years her junior: Jakob Ottesen.

I meet Knud in front of the Pompidou Center.

I give him the envelope, and we eat frog legs at a nearby restaurant.

—Strange country, isn't it?

—Yes, I say. I keep seeing that weird copy of St. Peter's in the middle of nowhere.

—Yes, it's terrible. But probably the most absurd part is that only 15% of the country's population is Christian.

Varvara and Jacob were married in the Marble Church in Bredgade one Saturday in August 1980 and separated on a Tuesday in December that same year. As a reason for the breakup they stated: irreconcilable differences.

—He could make me so damn furious, Varvara says. He'd look at me with eyes that said: *You are nothing. I think you're worthless.* And then I shouted at him and threw things at him, one time a five kilo Buddha figure, another time a bottle of Moët et Chandon. Our reconciliations were spectacular, but it was hard work. Then I discovered that he did coke, and I knew I couldn't do it anymore. One of Lucan's sons was a drug addict. I knew exactly what it was about. A year later I plunged equally headlong into marriage with Aage.

In the plane on the way home I open the envelope Knud just gave me.

It contains 10,000 Danish kroner in large bills.

Aage Jørgensen was a professor of Italian literature.

He had been the director of The Danish Institute at Via Omero for a number of years, and despite his rather satyr-like figure, he dressed and acted like Sicilian landed gentry.

—He was arrogant in such a wonderful way. He felt something, he knew something, he certainly pontificated much too much, but I ate it all up. His vulnerability was as obvious as his belly and snub-nose and made all of his posing and all of his mannerisms seem justified. It's not always easy to be oneself, is it? A sensitive, intelligent poseur is always preferable to one who is dumb, unfeeling, and natural!

They spent their honeymoon in Ravello, where Varvara's needs were attended to by a young servant while Aage slept off his benders.

Knirke and Mikael are in Berlin to interview a female TV journalist.

I get an email that evening:

When we called, she was in Hungary. We'll meet her tomorrow afternoon instead. How was your trip? I wonder whether Knud is aboveboard.

I respond that everything went well, and that I don't know whether or not Knud is above board.

In a way I'd rather not know.

The seventh time I visit Varvara, I ask a few of Gunilla's questions.

—Did you have a sunstroke or what?

I explain that Andreas has hired a journalist to help me out.

Varvara retreats to the other room and makes a phone call.

They talk for a long time.

—Forget those questions, she says when she returns. They'll have to live with what they get.

Jakob Ottesen died a year later of a heroin overdose in an apartment in Abel Cathrinesgade.

Aage Jørgensen died of prostate cancer two months later in a bed at Gentofte Hospital.

In January 1982, Varvara married Jaakko Tuominen, a middle-aged Finnish rally-driver whom she met at a New Year's party in Gotland, Sweden. He brought her along as his co-driver in the year's Paris-Dakar, and when she returned home from Senegal a few weeks later, she asked her lawyer to contact his.

—A man who can't handle losing is no man, she told her seven-year-old daughter.

I walk to the post office and pay my bills with Knud's money. I hide the rest in my book shelf behind *The Promised Land* and *A Fortunate Man*.

Knirke sends me a photograph of the TV journalist drinking caffe latte and talking on her cellphone.

The next day I see her on television.

She's standing in front of some trees at the bottom of an open mine somewhere in Hungary. They are eight million years old, she explains.

Knirke calls.

—Now we're in Swinoujscie, in Poland. The ferry to Ystad leaves in an hour. That means we'll have half a day together before I continue on to Scotland.

Varvara stopped marrying.

Not only because Leonard had begun to call her Lady of the Rings.

It was also because Jaakko, that same year, plowed into a moose at 125 mph.

It seemed futile and rather ruthless to keep at it.

She found a lover.

She found two.

They survived.

She landed some big film roles and a French bulldog.

Cille went for walks with the dog along with a girlfriend who lived on Hambros Allé and had a dachshund.

The dachshund's name was Amadeus.

The bulldog's name was Bibi.

The girlfriend's mother hit on Varvara, and Varvara thought: Why not?

They had an affair that summer and let kids be kids and dogs dogs.

They broke up amicably when her husband grew suspicious.

Varvara found another lover.

I'm cleaning the apartment when my sister calls. She says that it has been seven years since our mother died. We discuss our father.

—He's crushed, she says.

—It's his own fault, I say.

—I agree, but he's an old man.

—And?

—He doesn't understand much.

Varvara and Cille and Bibi moved to Frederiksberg.

Cille began at Barfoed's School, and Varvara began having an affair with her new doctor.

Bibi stopped eating.

Varvara's doctor was tall and gray-haired with a pencil mustache.

He was very meticulous about his clothing.

He had perfect nails.

After a few weeks Bibi became interested in the dogs at Frederiksberg Allé and rediscovered her appetite.

When later that fall Varvara had terrible pains in the small of her back, her lover wrote out a prescription for morphine.

It was so effective that Varvara continued to visit him long after his gentlemanly manners had begun to irritate her.

After about eight months, she finally broke things off with him, and her new doctor prescribed a stay at a drug treatment center.

Here she made friends with a truck driver from the town of Stege and read *The New Testament* for the first time in her life.

—I'd always avoided religion, actually. I felt there was something strangely screwed up about religious people. But suddenly I saw the beauty in it. I probably also needed to be seized by something else. And Tage was a real mensch. He meant so well. Religion was really a big help to him, and so we sat there drinking tea and chatting about the Acts of the Apostles and the Epistle to the Hebrews. It was really quite lovely. We embraced each other all the time up there.

Knirke and I embrace. I lift her up and carry her to the bed.

—Hold on, she says, I want to look at you a sec.

We look at each other.

—Okay, she says.

She tells me about the family they visited nine miles from Malmö. They live in a brand-new Hanseatic town with bumpy cobblestones and wrought iron street lights. The town is in the middle of a field.

She tells me about her mother, who just had surgery for breast cancer.

Knirke's father is a former high ranking civil servant but now raises sheep on the island of Møn. Her mother is a potter on another island, Anholt, and she's married to a boozy musician.

She asks about my parents.

I tell her my mother was a translator.

I tell her my father owns a small company that provides electronics for the windmill industry.

I don't tell her I've broken off relations with him.

Tage was trained as a gardener, and he offered to help when he heard about Varvara's rooftop terrace.

They went down to the local gardening association.

First she bought one book, then more, and before she knew it she was standing seventy-five feet up in the air cutting and watering and fertilizing.

Cille thought it was batshit crazy, but then Cille thought almost everything was batshit crazy.

She snapped at her teachers and spent most of her time gazing in the mirror.

—Tell me about Lucan, she said every now and then.

That was when things were going well.

Varvara no longer felt her back pain.

I get Gunilla's version of Varvara's first forty years. It fills precisely one hundred pages and consists of lightly edited transcriptions of the tapes.

I peruse the document.

All questions are gone, and the text appears like a cohesive, chronological report on Varvara's life as told by herself.

I get a text from Knirke:
Just landed
in Aberdeen.

Knud calls.

I run into Sune on the street.
—How about a beer? I say.
—Another time. I'm a little busy.
—It's okay, I say.
—I got your message, he says.
—What's wrong? I ask.
—I really don't have the time, he says.
—Say hello for me, I say.

I'm sitting on a British Airways flight.
I fall asleep and dream that I'm leading my father deep into the forest and then run away from him.

Varvara's popular breakthrough came as a brothel madam in the TV series "The Apartment Building."
She played Pinter and Norén.
She didn't tell her colleagues that she'd acted alongside the former.
She took care of her roses and got praised by the critics.
Cille survived puberty relatively unscathed and started school at Frederiksberg Gymnasium.
She didn't praise her mother, but she criticized her less.
Varvara went out now and then when she was invited, but mostly lived a quiet life.

She told herself she preferred it that way.
She told herself it was good for Cille.

I stare down at a soft, pastel-colored Johannesburg and can see houses made of corrugated sheets, scruffy dwarf trees, lines with clothes in bright colors, unleashed dogs, and a throng of pedestrians. Farther south are skyscrapers made of glass and steel and cement.

I zip right through customs.

I take a cab to a place called Sandton and check in at the hotel Knud asked me to use: Falstaff Inn.

I stay by the pool most of the day. I've brought my tape recorder and laptop.

Knirke sends a photograph of a golf course right next to the sea.
She writes that the Danish couple they've visited run a small hotel.
Now she's on her way to Dubai.
She writes that she's growing tired of Mikael's company.

I'll be happy when this trip is over.

At five o'clock, someone knocks on my door. A young Black woman in a pink Chanel suit enters.

She offers me her cool, slender hand and asks if she can use my bathroom.

She locks the door behind her and returns a minute later with a small white envelope.

I use my credit card to open the safe-deposit box in the closet and hand her the envelope I've brought along.

She returns to the bathroom.

Soon afterward, she leaves.

That evening, I eat corn soup and ostrich in the hotel restaurant, and twelve hours later I'm sitting in a cab on my way to the airport.

Varvara had started to feel a bit guilty.

Cille was 16 years old and seemed completely disinterested in the opposite sex.

She never went to parties with her classmates and usually spent her Saturday evenings studying.

She preferred math, chemistry, and physics.

Varvara tried in vain to get her to drink a glass of wine every now and then.

She thought: It's all been too much on her. *I have been too much.*

Varvara stopped drinking.

She read a book on Niels Bohr and another in English on the Indian mathematics genius Srinivasa Ramanujan.

She politely declined every kind of invitation.

The only thing that could lure Cille away from her books was *Beverly Hills 90210*, and Varvara made sure to be home when it was on.

She quickly learned not to comment on the boys' appearances.

All she would say was a little about the intrigue or, if necessary, the acting (only praise), then waited for Cille to speak.

She never did, though.

When Cille asked her for a pair of prescriptionless eyeglasses (because she thought it would help her grades), Varvara complied without hesitation.

Every now and then, as they sat silently across from each other at the dinner table, Varvara had to clutch the edge of the table and close her eyes for a moment.

When I get home, I find an unaddressed envelope under my door. It contains 10,000 kroner in cash.

I consider paying off a little of my debt to the unemployment office but decide that it's not worth the risk. Instead, I hide the envelope behind my unread copy of *Mason & Dixon*.

Knirke sends me a photo of the world's only seven-star hotel. It was built on a beach in the shape of a gigantic sail. There's an underwater restaurant, she writes, and a helicopter landing pad on the roof.

I send ten more pages to Andreas and Gunilla, and I deliver the latest tape to the publisher's office that very afternoon. I've decided to continue as if nothing had happened.

One day when the silence at the dinner table was especially oppressive, Varvara fell out of her chair.

Cille called for an ambulance, but the doctors at Frederiksberg Hospital could find nothing physically wrong with her.

They referred her to a psychiatrist.

He listened patiently to her account, then explained with a smile how they were in the midst of a minor epidemic.

He told her about a five-year old boy who'd arranged all of his matchbox cars in a row and given them parking tickets.

He told her about a wild and eccentric painter whose daughter had declared she wanted to be an accountant.

Knirke sends a photo of a Danish biologist and his African girlfriend. They're standing next to a red Toyota Land Cruiser. In the background, three giraffes glide past in mid-stride.

She tells me that she can see Zanzibar from her hotel room.

Would you like to go there with me some day?

There's nothing I'd rather do, I quickly reply. Are you doing anything tomorrow?

I call Andreas, but he's in a meeting.

I call Sune, but he doesn't answer the phone.

The eighth time I visit Varvara, she's beaming.

We sit on the striped sofa and eat chocolates from a small mahogany box.

—Are you into marzipan or nougat?

She tells me how she met Knud.

He bought a painting by a young female painter right out from underneath her nose.

—What an asshole! I thought.

As a gesture of goodwill, he asked if he could buy her a glass of champagne down in the café.

Later, he invited her to a picnic in Frederiksberg Garden.

He invited her to the Seychelles.

He invited her to a coffee shop.

He was half a head shorter than her, but he could do things with his face that made her laugh. He knew how to cook.

After a month, she said to him:

—I'll never move in with you, and I'll never marry you, but in every other way I am yours.

—I can live with that, he said.

A few weeks later, he showed up with the painting under his arm.

It's on the wall in her living room.

Andreas leaves a message on my answering machine:
—We're running out of time. Can you send me what you've got?

I print Knirke's photos and pin them on the wall.

When Knud calls, I tell him I need a break.

Varvara says:
—Sometimes we take a walk in the cemetery. Somewhere there's a gravestone that reads "Doctor in Slagelse" under the name. There's a family plot with a supreme court justice and a chief medical doctor; right between them is a gravestone that simply reads "human being." Honestly, I don't know which is more pretentious!

I'm working on the computer when I get an email from Knirke. She and Mikael are now in Beijing. They're going to interview a Danish visual artist.
Attached is a photo of a plate of food.
Take a guess: what is this? she asks.
Tenderloin? I write. Pigtail?

She doesn't respond.

The telephone rings the next morning shortly before nine.

—It's so awful, Varvara says. Do you know anything?

—About what? I say.

—It's in the newspaper today. It says that Knirke and that journalist were arrested. Something whacky about crickets or grasshoppers.

I call Knirke and get her voicemail.

I hurry down to the kiosk on Istedgade.

The wind is intense, and when I open up the newspaper, one section flies out of my hand.

With some difficulty, I unfold the newspaper and find what I'm looking for.

The headline reads: Two Danes arrested in China.

The embassy states that Knirke and Mikael were arrested during a raid at an illegal gambling site.

Emma calls half an hour later.

—Do you know anything more than what's in the newspaper?

I get an email from my writers' academy friend Jonas:

Johanne has started a blog. You should probably check it out: www.poetess.dk/blog

I call the Danish foreign ministry and speak to a man who tells me there's no news.

He refers me to a web page that provides general information on the conditions for foreigners in China.

He says I'm welcome to call again, but they can't promise to inform me of any developments in the case since I'm not related to either of the two involved.

On the web I find more than fifty articles on foreign journalists who have been arrested in China.

I find an article on crickets.

It says that cricket fighting is a thousand-year-old tradition, that the type of cricket most commonly used is *Velarifictorus micado*, a black or dark-brown variety that grows from between one-half-inch to a little less than one-inch long and is particularly territorial and aggressive by nature.

Knud calls:

—I know some people over there. I'll give them a call.

On September 14 Johanne writes on her blog:

Pelle No-Tail (5)

Once upon a time I had a boyfriend named Pelle. He wasn't quite well. One time when I accidentally burned the rice, he bound me to the radiator, and turned the heat all the way up. He stuffed a lemon in my mouth and sealed it with duct tape.

He slathered a baseball bat with salad dressing and shoved it up my asshole.

He said: So, you like it like that?

He dripped wax on my back.

He brought two prostitutes from Istedgade and asked one of them to hit me with an extension cord while he fucked the other one right in front of me.

He asked them to switch places.

He said: That'll teach you.

Pelle is a writer just like me.

You can find his books at the library.

His dick measures somewhere between four and six inches.

There are four other, similar posts. In one I force her to drink piss. In another I force her to be fucked by two Turkish boys at a public toilet. Every post begins with "Once upon a time I had a boyfriend named Pelle" and ends with "His dick measures somewhere between four and six inches."

I reply to Jonas:

Oh boy, poor Johanne. Don't you think people will see it for what it is?

I sit at the computer waiting for any sign of life.

On an English website I find an article by an American anthropologist.

At the top of page two I come across the sentence

"Recent crackdowns in the city have even led to executions."

The article is from last summer.

Varvara calls:

—Any news?

I tell her about what I'd just read.

—You'll have to go there and bring her back, she says.

I sit for a while staring at the blue house across the street.

Then I cross the room to the bookshelf and rummage behind the letter P.

I count my money.

At flightticket.dk I find a flight to Beijing that's departing the next day.

I download a visa application and take the S-train to Hellerup.

After standing in line for forty-five minutes, I pay a rush fee of 250 kroner and learn that I can pick up my visa the following day.

I call Knirke, and a woman answers the phone in Chinese.

In bad English she tells me that it's impossible to speak to the subscriber at this time.

Knud calls.

I can't sleep.

I'm trying on sunglasses in the duty-free shop when I catch sight of my father's bald dome down by security.

I put the sunglasses back on the rack and double check that it is him (he's reaching for his cotton coat, his laptop), and I hustle toward the gate.

In the terminal I go to the men's room.

Just as I sit down, I hear the door open.

—Pelle?

I sit stock still.

I consider lifting my feet.

—Pelle?

The restroom door opens again.

I remain seated for ten minutes, then head toward my gate, where people are boarding.

We have a layover in Budapest.

At the gate I call the Danish embassy in Beijing.

I speak to a female associate who has no news to share.

She doesn't sound thrilled that I'm on my way.

—This kind of thing requires swift diplomacy, and that's what we're doing. It was the ambassador himself who contacted the authorities.

I check my email.

There's a message from Jonas:

I don't know whether people will see it for what it is or not. Sometimes they would rather believe the worst because that's more entertaining.

I listen to Varvara's voice on the plane:

—Leonard's youngest, Veronika, plays the tuba. She's such a slight thing, with long, rust-colored hair. She performed recently with fourteen other tuba players. It sounded dreadful, but she looked so astonishing!

Leonard is the director of a record company and married to a former singer.

Elizabeth is an assistant professor of literature at Aarhus University.

She's married to a psychiatrist.

I have trouble concentrating.

Cille is nearly finished with her medical degree.

I have some articles in my bag that I've printed off the Internet, among them the one from the English website.

The American anthropologist describes a place where crickets are locked up for five days before the fight so they can't be doped.

Men in white lab coats and masks weigh them, since there can only be a 40 mg difference between the two combatants.

A man by the name of Mr. Wu explains that one must not smoke, drink, eat, talk, make noise, or wear aftershave during a fight.

The article describes how the trainers wear white cotton gloves.

They place their crickets at each end of the miniature arena.

The referee takes bets, and bids are made, from 100 yuan and up.

When the referee asks the trainers to prepare the crickets, the room hushes.

The two trainers incite their crickets with a blade of grass.

They stroke their back legs, jaws, and spine.

—Open the gate! The judge cries, and an assistant raises the plate that divides the arena.

Seated to my left an elderly, nearly white-haired Chinese man in dark-blue pants and yellow-brown shoes.

To my right sits an eastern European businessman wearing a green silk tie and gold cufflinks.

I read about Jia Sidao, a prime minister in the Song Dynasty. He lived from 1213 to 1275 and wrote *The Book of Crickets*. He was so obsessed with crickets that his kingdom fell apart and was invaded by the Mongols.

I eat the goulash that is served.

Jia Sidao names five virtues shared by crickets and humans:

He sings when it's time to sing: That's reliability.

When he meets an enemy, he does not hesitate: That's courage.

Even when he's badly wounded, he will not surrender: That's loyalty.

When he is defeated, he will not sing: He knows shame.

When he is freezing cold, he goes home: He's sensible and faces the facts.

Varvara says:

—My relationship with the truth has probably not always been a very close one.

It's early afternoon when I arrive.

As soon as we get out of the plane, I turn on my cell phone.

I call Knirke, but she doesn't answer. I hang up before the Chinese woman switches to English.

I call the embassy and talk to a male associate who speaks Danish in a slightly affected, old-fashioned way. He tells me there is no news.

I give him my telephone number and let him know where I'm staying.

I take a taxi.

I've never been to China.

The air is thick with smog and swinging cranes.

I see some men on a street corner leaning over a board game.

I see an elderly woman getting her hair cut.

A man lies sleeping on a cargo bike.

The hotel I've booked is called Zhong'an and is within walking distance to Tiananmen Square and The Forbidden City.

I check in and call the Danish visual artist that Knirke and Mikael interviewed.

She says she's in Hong Kong.

She says the friend who'd escorted them on the evening they were arrested does not wish to be contacted.

He's afraid of attracting the attention of the authorities.

I retrieve a scrap of paper Knud gave me. I open the money belt and make sure that the small envelope I am to deliver is still there.

The ambassador is a tall, smiling man with blond hair. He offers me a cup of coffee and a vanilla cookie.

He figures everything will work itself out, he says.

—Unfortunately, the timing isn't so great. With the Olympics over, the authorities have returned to their old ways. It's just like with children: They can be polite for only so long.

He explains that the crux of the matter is whether Mikael and Knirke gambled or just watched the fight.

He says that the incident will, in just a few days, turn from being a diplomatic affair to being a political one.

He says the Chinese understand that.

He says the Danish government is briefed regularly.

He shrugs when I ask if there's anything I can do.

He says:

—The Chinese authorities are not to be messed with.

A defeated cricket leaves the arena without protest.

A cricket fights better if it has sex before a fight.

It is the female that mounts the male.

Unable to hail a taxi, I take a rickshaw instead. I sit beneath a red baldachin with gold fringe as a boy of sixteen or seventeen stamps hard on the pedals. He has an exclamation point of sweat along his spine.

After a quarter of an hour, he stops in front of a large jewelry shop, and I pay him a little more than what he asks for.

There's a guard just inside the door.

I show him the note and I'm escorted through the enormous shop and into a backroom where four or five men are playing cards.

We walk through a kitchen, up a narrow staircase, and halt in front of a broad, ornately carved door.

The guard knocks, and a moment later there's a subdued command from inside.

A small man with buzzed hair and thick shoulder pads stands at the window gazing down at the street.

He turns and approaches me.

We shake hands.

—So you are Knud's friend? he says.

He barks out the k and pronounces the d like a t.

—Please sit.

I sit on a wooden chair with a large, circular armrest and a square seat upholstered in faded red leather.

He sits down behind a giant desk.

—First time China? he says and offers me a cup of tea.

I tell him why I'm in the country.

—Ah, crickets serious business. Gambling serious business.

He looks out the window.

Next to the desk is a statue of a warrior with a red face and a long beard.

He's armed with something that resembles a halberd.

My host sips from his tea, and I do the same.

Then he says:

—I believe you have something for me?

I fumble with the money belt and pull out the envelope.

I hand it to him.

He smiles.

—Knud is a very good friend of mine.

Before I leave, he hands me a white envelope on which are written some Chinese characters.

I eat at the hotel.

Varvara says:

—I was much better at arguing in English. It's as if the Danish language puts a damper on everything.

I get an email from my father.

He's in San Diego.

He would like to see me.

I delete it and go to bed.

It is 8:30 p.m. Chinese time.

My cell phone rings: It lights up on the nightstand and vibrates across the table.

—Did I wake you? Andreas says.

—No, no you didn't.

—Will we get the last tape soon? We've almost run out of time, and Gunilla can get no farther.

—Something has come up, I say, but I'm almost done. I'll send it to you in the next few days.

—Send it tomorrow, he says. Or even better: Bring it here.

—I'll try to make it.

I drink espresso and eat egg and bacon in the hotel restaurant.

I show the white envelope to the receptionist, and she marks an X on a little map.

I head east through the city on foot.

I pass a park where 10-15 couples dance on a small gravel square.

I pass a military truck parked in front of a television retail store.

Outside a small shop two men sit drinking beer.

They laugh and I see that one of them is missing a front tooth.

I walk into a glass-covered skyscraper.

Uniformed men are seated in a row behind a marble counter, and I show the envelope to the first one who's available.

He grabs his telephone and asks me to fill out a form with my name and address, etc.

A moment later, he prints out a small pass for me.

My ears pop.

The elevator stops at the 44th floor, and I climb out.

I show my pass to a guard, who raises his right arm and points. I pass a row of closed doors and enter a high-ceilinged room with a skylight.

There's a staircase and a gallery made of dark wood and steel.

A woman with gold eyeglasses asks me to sit.

I wait.

A young woman in high heels descends the stairs.

She's wearing a white silk blouse.

She's wearing dark-red, almost liver-colored lipstick.

She offers her hand.

—Please, she says.

The office is empty.

She asks me to sit in a deep leather sofa and fetches me a cup of tea.

—Mr. Xun will be here in a moment, she says with a clear American accent.

She leaves.

I stand and go to the window.

I can see a zoo and a group of older, colorful buildings that I figure must be the Forbidden City.

There's a humongous stadium.

There are mountains in the background.

Mr. Xun arrives twenty minutes later.

He places the envelope in the inner pocket of his blue suit without opening it.

He tells me that he was once in Denmark.

—Very beautiful, he says. Hans Christian Andersen. Agriculture. Windmills.

He asks me what I do for a living.

—Me too, he says excitedly.

He gathers five beautifully bound books off a shelf to the right of the desk.

A red, a green, a yellow, a blue, and a purple.

—Poems, he says and smiles. I am a poet.

When I begin to tell him about Knirke, he interrupts.

—Your first name, please?

He writes in one of the books, the purple.

He hands it to me and says that, unfortunately, he has to go.

I open the book when I'm in the elevator.

The inscription is in Chinese.

I pass a market on my way home.

I wander around aimlessly among flowers, wicker furniture, fish, spices, toys, meat, vegetables, cell phones, leather goods, and find at last a booth with crickets.

A row of clay pots stands in tight formation on small

rickety tables. Customers file past, lift a lid, and bait the insect with a straw, or shine a flashlight on it.

One is chosen, and a large wad of bills changes hands.

Others are sold in bamboo boxes on the cheap, five at a time.

I lift a lid and am amazed at how small the insect is.

At a booth a little farther down, men are clustered around a small Plexiglas container watching a cricket fight.

The two crickets tear at one another with their jaws.

One is knocked on its back.

It gets to its feet immediately.

Like two wrestlers, they grasp at each other with their forelegs.

One leaps over the other.

The other whirls around.

Suddenly one withdraws, and the other begins to sing: an arrhythmic, monotonous sound much like a cicada, only higher pitched. The loser is thrown into a plastic bucket, and an intense auction follows before the winner is sold to a man in a striped shirt.

I try calling Knirke.

I try calling the Danish visual artist.

I eat shark fin soup at a small restaurant.

When I ask the receptionist whether she can translate Mr. Xun's inscription, she smiles politely.

She clutches the book with her long, slightly curved fingers and all of a sudden seems a little worried.

She finds her smile once more and says:

—A friend of a friend of a friend is also a friend.

Varvara says:

—Have you ever read anything by Spinoza? I read a biography about him a few years ago. What a thrilling man! He argued for freedom of religion and tolerance, and boy, did everyone hate him! He had such a fine, rather melancholy face.

The next morning, I call the embassy.

The man with the affected Danish tells me there are complications. The authorities have now officially charged Mikael and Knirke with gambling. Several witnesses claim they saw them making bets.

I ask to speak with the ambassador and am told to call again in the afternoon.

For a moment I stand on the sidewalk in front of the hotel before I head north. There's no breeze, and a tofu-white smog covers the city. I notice a man in a dark-green suit standing on the other side of the street reading a newspaper.

I enter Tiananmen Square.

A security camera is fastened way up on a light pole, and a policeman is rummaging through a younger man's bag.

On the way to Mao's mausoleum, I notice two delivery vans with tinted windows.

I don't see a single bench.

The smog is so thick I can't see the buildings at the far end of the square.

It's ten o'clock, and there are more than 100 people waiting in line.

Some are tourists, but most are Chinese, and judging by their blue work clothes, they're mostly from the provinces.

When I turn around, I see the man in the dark-green suit standing ten feet behind me.

He's wearing sunglasses with light blue-lenses.

He's about my age.

The building is more than 600 feet long and 600 feet wide.

There's a booth in the enormous vestibule where one can purchase a small flower wrapped in cellophane.

We enter a hall with a white marble statue of Mao seated on a chair.

There's a large wall painting of a Chinese landscape.

Many fall to their knees and lay flowers at his feet.

We file past the glass casket in two rows.

The uniformed guards make sure that the line keeps moving.

I barely manage to see that Mao's skin has turned orange.

I buy *Little Red Book* in English translation and sit down at a café.

My shadow sits a few tables away.

I eat a club sandwich and drink Chinese beer.

"In waking a tiger, use a long stick," says Chairman Mao.

He has been dead for more than 30 years.

He's lying under a red cloth.

He spends most of the time in a nuclear safe freezer.

He says: "The guerilla must move amongst the people as a fish swims in the sea."

I call the Danish artist.

She doesn't answer the phone.

I call the ambassador and manage to arrange a meeting for the following day.

I return to the hotel.

From the window I can see my shadow standing on the street below.

I order room service.

—Have you noticed, Varvara says, that artists always talk about money, while people with money always talk about art?

Chairman Mao says:
"There is in fact no such thing as art for art's sake."

He says:
"To read too many books is harmful."

I watch Chinese television.

I find an English-language station and watch a long report on cucumbers.

By crossing a cucumber with a pumpkin, the Chinese have developed a particularly hardy variety that can grow in greenhouses during the winter.

The program's background music reminds me of the kind you hear in American TV commercials.

I look out and discover that my shadow is gone.

Just as I fall asleep there's a knock at my door.
I'm naked.
I open the door a few inches and peer out.

I throw it open entirely.

—Are you okay? I say a moment later.

—Yes, Knirke says. I just wanted to see if you were serious about me.

— And seriously?

—They were a little rough with Mikael, but they didn't do anything to me. I just need something proper to eat.

I begin putting on my clothes.

—Not yet, she says. It can wait. Come here.

We eat cellophane noodles and drink Heineken.

Knirke tells me about the women she met in prison.

One was a prostitute.

Another had filed a complaint against a high-ranking public official.

A third had been interviewed by a Polish journalist.

We are the only customers in the restaurant.

—How did you even find me? I ask.

—A man from the embassy picked us up. He drove me here.

—And what about the charges?

—They were suddenly dropped.

—And Mikael?

—He's traveling to Nagasaki tomorrow. I told him I wasn't going.

On the Internet we find a cheap flight on Alitalia.

—Maybe what we need is a few days in Rome? Knirke says.

In Trastavere, I walk to a post office and mail the last of the tapes to Andreas.

A few hours later I send him an email with my final manuscript: Varvara's life told in forty pages.

—Tell me about your family, Knirke says that evening as we're sitting on Piazza de Renzi.

We drink prosecco.

—I don't quite know where to start, I say.

The waiter, a chubby man with a pouty mouth and long bangs, lays the cutlery in the center of our table.

He puts a veal cutlet next to Knirke and a lamb cutlet next to me.

We switch.

Soon he brings us salads.

—My mother died of cancer, I tell her. Seven years ago.

—Okay? Knirke says.

She looks directly at me.

—What about your father?

—I have no contact with him. He left my mother when she got sick. He met a woman twenty years younger and he's still with her.

—Oh God, Knirke says.

I nod.

One week later, I see Johanne and Andreas arm in arm on their way down Vesterbrogade.

I wave at them.

Maybe it's time to change publishers? I think to myself.

The ninth time I visit Varvara I take Knirke with me.

Knud is making dinner when we arrive, and Knirke goes to the kitchen and helps him finish.

Varvara sits on the striped sofa drinking a mojito while I set the table and walk back and forth between the kitchen and the living room.

—I've read your little book, by the way, she says.

—Yeah? I say while placing a long-stemmed glass. Did Andreas send you the manuscript?

—He sent yours and Gunilla's versions. Gunilla's is terribly dull, but he says that's the one people want.

—That's probably true.

—I suggested publishing both, but they don't want to do that, of course.

She raises her green drink to her mouth.

—But if you would like, maybe you can just change the names and publish it as fiction? That would be all right with me.

I look at a large Chinese vase on the table, decorated

with two fish, one turquoise and the other the color of apricots.

—Thanks, I say. I'll think about it.

I go to the kitchen to get the bottle of white wine Knud has opened.

Knirke's busy pouring mussels into a large bowl.

Knud hands me a plate with rough-cut, homemade French fries.

—I guess we're ready, he says.

Varvara Eng has eight grandchildren.

She has a lover who may or may not be aboveboard.

She has a friend who is a truck driver and lives in the town of Stege.

He says:

—Jesus is your friend, Varvara, don't you forget.

He examines her roses for aphids.

She has a career that is over, and four children, of which she sees only three.

It could be much worse.

It could be all of them.

It could be one big misunderstanding.

It could be lonely.

It could be empty.

It is not, though.

She has a rooftop terrace from which she can see Søndermarken, Frederiksberg Garden, and most of Vesterbro.

The poem by Per Højholt on p. 70
was originally published in Danish in
PRAKSIS 8: Album, *tumult* (1989).

A source from which I have drawn
information: Hugh Raffles' "Cricket
Fighting" in *Granta* 98, Summer 2007.

SF

SIMON FRUELUND is a Danish author who debuted in 1997 with the story collection *Milk* (US edition 2013). Since then he has published another story collection, four short novels, among them *Civil Twilight* (US edition 2013), and a poetry collection. From 1997 to 2006 he worked as an editor at the publisher Gyldendal. Since 2012 he has taught creative writing at Vallekilde Højskole. *The World and Varvara* is his third book translated into English.

K.E. Semmel is a writer and translator. His translations include novels by, among others, Naja Marie Aidt, Karin Fossum, Simon Fruelund, and Jussi Adler Olsen. He is a former Literary Translation Fellow from the National Endowment for the Arts. His debut novel, *The Book of Losman*, is forthcoming in 2024 from SFWP. Visit him online at kesemmel.com